LANNIGAN'S STAR

When Lannigan rode into Plainsville he found a town ready to explode. The railroad was coming and men were fighting for the chance to make big money. Lannigan wanted only to ride on; his hard fists and ready guns had already brought him enough trouble. But when the past caught up with him, he had no option but to settle his debts, even if this meant that once more he was the lone target of powerful and evil men. Lannigan knew it was kill or be killed!

JACK EDWARDES

LANNIGAN'S STAR

Complete and Unabridged

LINFORD
Leicester

First published in Great Britain in 1999 by
Robert Hale Limited
London

First Linford Edition
published 2001
by arrangement with
Robert Hale Limited
London

British Library CIP Data

Edwardes, Jack
    Lannigan's star.—Large print ed.—
Linford western library
    1. Western stories
    2. Large type books
    I. Title
    823.9'14 [F]

ISBN 0–7089–9718–X

Published by
F. A. Thorpe (Publishing)
Anstey, Leicestershire

Set by Words & Graphics Ltd.
Anstey, Leicestershire
Printed and bound in Great Britain by
T. J. International Ltd., Padstow, Cornwall

This book is printed on acid-free paper

1

Lannigan was on the coach road about ten miles south of Plainsville when he saw the riderless horse, about a third of a mile to his east. Outlined against the bunch and buffalo grass, the animal had its head down, rubbing at its foreleg. Lannigan eased himself down in his saddle, glad to take a break from the hard riding. He let the reins fall to the grey's neck, and pushed the sweat-stained hat back from his forehead. Lines creased the sides of his eyes as he looked across towards the riderless horse.

'Easy there, boy,' he muttered, as the grey shifted on the hard ground of the trail.

The riderless horse, nibbling at the grass between a creek and a stand of birch, probably belonged to some cowpoke grabbing a quiet smoke, he decided. But hell, there was no harm in checking it out. One day he'd maybe find himself on the ground after his horse had spooked, his lips dry with thirst, just hoping that some stranger would come riding by. He shifted around in his saddle and reached back to loosen the buckles of his saddle-bag. Rummaging around beneath a woollen workshirt he hauled out his old Army spyglass. Its metal was badly dented but Lannigan knew that the lenses were still true. Raising the spyglass he gave the eyepiece a couple of turns before bringing the riderless horse into focus.

The horse was a fine animal, not the scrubby range mount Lannigan had expected to see, and it now seemed intent only on filling its belly, shaking its head every few moments to free the loose reins. Lannigan could see that the animal wasn't hobbled. Its gait was even as it moved across the grass.

A short distance beyond the horse he could see a fold in the ground by the creek which might have kept a man hidden from his view. He held his spyglass steady on the fold for a few moments but could see nothing which might explain the horse. Only the water lapping at stiff reeds around the creek moved in his eyepiece. A small shift of his hands brought the spyglass on to the stand of birch over to the right of the grazing horse. At this time of the year the leaves weren't thick enough to provide cover, and neither men nor horses stood among the silver trunks.

Most likely there was a simple explanation. Maybe the horse had broken out of a corral in Plainsville. But then why was it saddled? Lannigan lowered the spyglass, a frown marking his weatherbeaten face. He eased his Peacemaker in its holster, held to his hip by a thonged tie-down. Just one quick look wouldn't delay him. He twisted around to push the spyglass into the bottom of his saddle-bag, and refastened the buckles. Then he picked up his reins and touched his heels to the flanks of his grey.

He was about half-way to the creek when he saw the patch of blue clothing mostly hidden behind the fold in the ground. Instantly, Lannigan checked his horse's lope, and took the reins in one hand, leaving his right hand free. Even close to a town it could still be dangerous to come on a man without warning.

'Howdy, stranger,' he called.

There was no sign of movement from the blue clothing. He urged his grey forward again, and as he drew level with the grazing horse he could see that the blue patch of colour on the ground belonged to a rain slicker. Had he come off the coachroad for some old cowboy sleeping off a drunk? The grazing horse, its hindquarters lathered with sweat, snickered gently, but then went back to nibbling the grass. The slicker remained still. The man was face down, one arm bent beneath his head, the other thrown out in the direction of the creek. Lannigan slid on to the springy ground, sizing up the situation.

The slicker moved in a tremor, and for several seconds there came the noise which always reminded Lannigan of somebody who'd gotten tobacco juice in his windpipe. Then the slicker was still again and Lannigan knew he'd just seen another man die.

As if taking a real interest in the newcomers for the first time, the grazing horse lifted its head again and inspected him with marble-brown eyes before ambling across and thrusting a dew-soaked muzzle into his shirt. Out of habit he raised his cupped hand to allow the horse to lick off his sweat while he looked around him. Save for a jack rabbit which showed its head by a birch, nothing moved. In the peace of the meadow, with water bubbling in the creek, and the light wind sighing through the trees, it wasn't a bad place to die, Lannigan decided. That's if the stranger was ready for death. His horse shifted behind him but the animals were comfortable with each other and he let the reins fall over the grey's head.

Thick woollen trousers covered the dead man's legs and he'd favoured handmade boots with rows of coloured stitching. Unless he'd got lucky in a poker game he'd been no rangeman, he decided; a townsman, maybe, who should have stuck to the stagecoach. Lannigan knelt on the ground, grasping the slicker to heave over what had once been a heavily built man. He grunted with the effort, causing the two horses to raise their heads from the grass. But save for a glance, Lannigan paid them no attention. Instead, he looked down at the mess of blood which had blackened the front of the slicker. Blood still oozed from the two bullet wounds in the man's chest. Lannigan reckoned he'd maybe taken a couple of hours to die. He sank back on his heels.

'Wish to hell I'd stuck to the coach road,' he said aloud.

If he'd found the stranger in open plain he'd have buried him and ridden on. Hell, he might even have told the next sheriff he came across what he'd done. But this was different. Only ten miles from Plainsville anybody could come riding by, and maybe the stage was due this way. Folks would be asking questions if he just rode on. The body could be of an important man from Plainsville, and if the townsfolk kicked up a commotion and the law came looking they might not trouble to look too far for someone to hang.

'Seems a man can't stay out of trouble even if he tries,' again Lannigan spoke aloud as he got to his feet.

He went over to the dead man's horse, took up the loose reins, and led the horse towards the body. As the scent of blood rose to its nostrils the animal jerked its head away from Lannigan's hand, but he had anticipated this, and he leaned back, digging a heel into the ground. He waited until the horse had steadied, then holding on to the reins with one hand, he shoved at the animal's hindquarters with the other, all the while talking to the horse in a soft voice. When he was satisfied that the animal was in the position he wanted, and the horse was settled, he dropped the reins over its head, and took down the stranger's lariat.

Nowadays he rarely used his own forty feet of hemp but what he was about to do was one task he knew he was unlikely to forget. Dropping to one knee, he took the dally-end, turned it around the handstitched boots and tied a bowline. The fold in the ground made his next task easier than it might have been. He scrabbled his hands and arms beneath the body, flexed his broad shoulders, filled his lungs with air, and heaved. As he took the weight he turned quickly on the heel of his boot and lifted the dead man across the saddle of the horse. The instant the weight went off Lannigan's arms and shoulders his hand snaked out and grasped the reins before the horse could skitter away from him. But whoever had broken the stranger's horse knew his job. A raised hoof and a slight shake of the head were the animal's only movements as the body slumped across the saddle.

Breathing heavily, Lannigan threw the rope beneath the horse's belly, moved around to the other flank and secured the man's hands. The remaining length of hemp he lashed to the horn of the saddle. His own horse had moved to the richer grass nearer the creek but at Lannigan's whistle it jerked up its head and trotted across. With his own reins in one hand, Lannigan hoisted himself into the saddle. With the other hand he held the stranger's horse, moving his grey forward slowly until the leading reins grew taut, then allowing them to slacken as the dead man's horse moved forward with the grey.

He sure hadn't counted on coming across a killing but he knew there was no going back. He'd deliver the stranger to the local sheriff, rest up for a day, and be on his way north. He'd maybe have to answer a few questions, but he felt easier knowing he was a long way from Kansas. Anyways, the townsfolk would likely know why the stranger was killed, could maybe guess already who'd done it, he figured. Some feud over land or a fight over a woman. Maybe the dead stranger was a tinhorn who'd dealt a wrong card once too often.

Then Lannigan swore softly, angry with himself. Was this what he'd come to? Grabbing any notion at the first sign of trouble? Don't be a god-damned fool, he told himself. Life dealt out the cards and all a man could do was play them the best he could. The hard times were behind him. Finding this feller bushwhacked was just plumb bad luck. After a week had passed most of the townsfolk of Plainsville would have forgotten he existed. If anyone gave him a thought they'd remember him just as a passing stranger who chanced across a dead man close to their town. There was no need to get hogtied. But no matter how much he tried to reason with himself Lannigan couldn't shake off his uneasiness as he turned the grey's head back towards the coach road and the ride into Plainsville.

2

Lannigan had left the trail and was twenty yards down Main Street when the crowd began to gather. Townsfolk came out of stores to gape, some of the women in dresses shipped from the East, high-button boots showing beneath their hems. Other women wore plain cotton dresses which swept the boardwalks. A handful of men wore suits and derby hats, others wore working clothes beneath dusty aprons. Lannigan kept his eyes ahead. There'd be plenty of time for questions, he reckoned. Half-way down the street, a pretty red-haired young woman driving herself in a buggy turned her head away as Lannigan passed. A few yards later a couple of cowhands on wiry quarter-horses reined in to watch him ride by. Over to his right a blacksmith stepped out from the flames and steam of his forge, sweat gleaming on his face.

'You got a sheriff or a marshal here?' Lannigan called to him.

'Fifty yards past the saloon, Sheriff Hudson,' the blacksmith called back.

The word of his arrival must have spread along the boardwalks fast. By the time he reached level with the saloon half a dozen old-timers stood in front of the batwing doors, beer glasses in their hands. Lannigan licked his lips. A couple of beers would sure taste fine. On the balcony above the saloon front, three hurdy-gurdy girls, their rouged faces garish in the sunshine, leaned over for a better view of the body. Their voices, high with excitement, sounded strange in Lannigan's ears after his months on the trail.

'Damned near like the vaudeville in Dodge,' he muttered as his grey covered the last twenty yards to the sheriff's office.

A hatless grey-haired man with a star on his leather vest stood waiting on the boardwalk. Alongside him was a bony old-timer wearing a battered derby and faded dungarees. The man with the star stepped down from the boardwalk as Lannigan halted his grey at the hitching post.

'Howdy stranger. You got trouble there?'

'Not my trouble, Sheriff,' Lannigan said. 'Found him by the creek ten miles south. Took a couple of slugs to the chest.'

'I ain't the sheriff, son. Thank the good Lord,' the grey-haired man said, glancing at the ivory handle of Lannigan's Peacemaker. 'Sheriff's away right now talking with the schoolmarm. Deputy Charley Ford's my name. Sheriff Hudson'll be back awhile.'

He moved around the two horses to get a good look at the dead man's face. 'This feller ain't from these parts, that's for sure. Looks kinda well-heeled, don't he?' Ford looked up at Lannigan who was resting easily in his saddle. 'This his hoss?'

'I guess so,' Lannigan said.

14

Ford nodded, and turned to call up to the oldtimer.

'Skinny, you get him across to Sam Bates. I want him laid out proper. This here could be an important man and there's no tellin' what's goin' to happen.'

'Sure, Charley!' The battered derby bobbed up and down with the oldtimer's excitement. He came down the steps on to the street and took the reins from Ford.

'The sheriff'll need everything from this poor feller's pockets. An' tell Sam to keep his nose out of anythin' he finds!' Ford turned back to Lannigan and jerked a thumb in the direction of the office.'Sheriff'll want to ask you some questions.'

'I could use a bath and some clean clothes.'

'Sure you could. But there's plenty of time for that,' Ford said. 'How do folk know you?'

'The name's Lannigan,' he said as he tethered his grey to the post.

He guessed Ford was treating him no worse and no better than he would any stranger who might have brought in a man dead from gunshot wounds. Until the sheriff was satisfied with his own story his chances of just riding through the town weren't worth a wooden nickel.

'Take that chair over there,' Ford said, when they were inside the office. The deputy glanced up at the battered clock on the whitewashed wall. 'Henry'll be back in a couple of minutes.'

Lannigan looked up suddenly from adjusting a spur. Maybe he'd be riding through, after all. 'Henry Hudson's the sheriff? Tall *hombre*, broken nose, favours a cross-draw?'

'That's the feller,' Ford said. 'Worn the badge here for nigh on ten years. Old Cavalry man. Rode out of Wilderness with just a scratch, he once told me.'

Lannigan's face broke into a broad grin. Only Henry Hudson would describe a Minié from a Johnny Reb carbine as just a scratch.

'Sergeant Henry Hudson! I'll be goddamned!'

On Lannigan's final words the door from the boardwalk opened. A man in his mid-fifties, nearly six-and-a-half feet tall, with a bent nose below a weather-stained brown hat, ducked beneath the door entrance. On his left hip was holstered a Colt with its butt pointing away from his belt. A grim smile emerged from below his curled moustaches.

'I'd gamble on that, Studs Lannigan. Yes, sir, I sure would!'

Lannigan had stood up from his chair as the sheriff entered, and the two men shook hands vigorously, clapping each other on the back.

'See you still got those crazy moustaches!'

'And you got rid of that goddamned studded belt!' Hudson said.

'Lost it to a tinhorn in Dodge,' Lannigan said. 'Kept the name, though!'

Hudson tossed his hat on to a rough table and sat down behind his desk. 'Heard you had some trouble down that way,' he said.

Lannigan kept the broad grin on his face. Henry hadn't changed, that was for sure. Still as straight as an arrow. Stood to reason that he hadn't hung on to that badge for ten years just talkin' with schoolmarms. He'd best be straight with Henry, then. Anyways, the old feller knew too much about him. Knew Lannigan had put on the blue shirt of the Cavalry a year too young. Kicked Lannigan's butt until he'd made a good trooper. Even pinned the chevrons on his sleeve when men were getting mowed down at the bloodbath of Wilderness.

'Coupla years in the brig,' Lannigan said finally. 'Killed a feller in a gunfight.'

Hudson stuck his boots on his desk. 'Don't sound much like Dodge,' he said. 'Providin' it was a fair fight.'

'I got railroaded. Turned out his old

18

man owned one of the biggest spreads thereabouts.'

Hudson took out the makings for a smoke. 'Never get tangled up with rich folks,' he said. He sprinkled tobacco from a small linen bag on to brown paper. 'Talkin' of rich folks, Studs,' he said, 'this feller you brought in from Beaver Creek looks as though he wasn't wanting for much.' Hudson waved a large hand in the direction of Ford. 'Saw Skinny and all the commotion around Sam Bates's place,' he explained. 'Took a look 'fore I got back.'

He rolled the smoke and lit it with a wooden match flicked across the sole of his boot. A moment later a cloud of blue smoke drifted up to the lamp hanging over the desk. All the time he kept his eyes on Lannigan.

'Saw his boots,' Lannigan said. 'But I've seen cowhands who'd blow six month's pay on hand-stitched boots.'

'You got somethin' there. Guess we'll know more when Sam's emptied his pockets.' Hudson sucked in smoke. 'So what brings you to this part of the country?'

'Just passin' through. Got some kinfolk up north. I'm aimin' to start all over.'

'Still followin' that star you were always on about?' Hudson looked at him thoughtfully. 'So Bart Hermann didn't get you up here?'

'Who the hell's Bart Hermann?'

'Charley, tell Lannigan about Bart Hermann.'

'Hermann's Bar-T is the biggest spread hereabouts,' Ford said. 'Over a hundred men on his payroll. More when they shift beef to the railhead. Bart Hermann sneezes and Plainsville catches a fever.'

'Well, I've never heard of him,' Lannigan said. 'An' I guess the name Studs Lannigan ain't worth a nickel to a rich man like him.'

'Could be worth a lot more to him if you can handle that sidearm,' said Ford.

'Not that we would want a feller like you takin' up with Hermann,' added Hudson quietly.

Lannigan felt the muscles in his jaw tighten. Sure, he was glad to see Henry Hudson again after all these years. And he hoped there'd be the chance to talk over old times. He and Henry had been through some mighty good times together. But right now all he wanted was to get his horse fed, and then get some honest grub into himself. The dead man was the town's business. He'd brought him in for a decent burial, that's all.

'Why the hell should I want to take up with a feller I've never heard of?' he asked.

'Listen, Studs. This town's sittin' on a powder keg,' Hudson replied. 'The railroad branch off the Union Pacific'll be here in a couple of years, an' by then Hermann seems set to own most of the town. Some mighty decent folks have quit Plainsville. An' there's a whole passel of trigger-happy varmints out at the Bar-T.'

'You know I ain't trigger-happy, Henry. And I ain't here for Hermann.'

He stood up. 'I ain't going nowheres. I'm gonna rest my horse and get some decent chow. But after a coupla days I'd like to be on my way north. Sounds like you should be askin' questions out at this Bar-T spread.'

Hudson swung his boots down from the desk.

'You'll find Widow Powell's place at the southern end of town. The grub's good and she don't charge much. Tell her I sent you.'

'Thanks. Gimme the day to rest up and we'll get together. Buy you some decent whiskey.'

'Sure thing,' the sheriff said, getting up from his chair, and turning to Ford. 'Guess I'll ride out and take a look down Beaver Creek.'

Outside in the street Lannigan had mounted his grey when he spotted a small man in a dusty black suit walking quickly towards him. As he drew closer

Lannigan could see that he was carrying a sheaf of papers and what looked like a small leather pocket-book. The man glanced briefly at Lannigan, gave a short nod, and stepped up on to the boardwalk to enter the sheriff's office. For a moment Lannigan was tempted to dismount and follow the man he guessed was Sam Bates. Then he shrugged. What the hell? His old sergeant was damned right. When he'd tangled with rich folks down in Kansas he'd finished up breaking rocks. He touched his heels to the grey.

'Time you and me got some chow,' he said aloud.

He trotted his grey down Main Street aware of the small group of men stood around Bates's Funeral Parlour. A couple of them turned to look at him as he drew level, but Lannigan kept his eyes ahead and his grey at a quiet trot. After taking advice from an old man who sat on his porch warming himself in the midday sun, he finally found Widow Powell's boarding house. A

23

whitewashed fence separated the two-storey clapboard from the dirt street, and a short path beyond the fence led through a small yard to an open door. By the time he'd secured his grey to the hitching post in front of the fence, a stern-faced woman dressed in black bombazine had appeared at the door. Lannigan pushed open the gate, taking off his hat as he walked up the path to where she stood.

'Name's Lannigan, ma'am. Sheriff Hudson said I might get a bed here for a coupla nights.'

'I'll have a room empty shortly, Mr Lannigan.' Her sharp eyes examined him from head to foot. 'Rules of the house are plain. Number one, payment in advance. Number two, no drinkin' under this roof. If you come back stinkin' drunk you sleep in the lean-to. Number three, any sidearms to be unloaded. Number four, breakfast at six sharp, and supper's at five or you go hungry.'

'Tell me, ma'am,' Lannigan said, his

face expressionless. 'Do I have to take my boots off in bed?'

Her eyebrows lifted an inch. 'Cowboy! You'd better be sure . . . '

She stopped suddenly, her generous lips quivering into what Lannigan thought might have been a smile.

'As sassy as the late Mr Powell! OK, put your saddle and your stuff in the lean-to. Jackson's livery stable'll look after your horse.'

She wrinkled her sharp nose. 'You've been on the trail sometime, I guess, Mr Lannigan?'

'Sure have, ma'am.'

'Then you'd better take a bath before you step through this door. Anytime after a couple hours.'

She shut the door firmly in his face. Lannigan grinned. There were women in this world a man'd never get the better of. He spent a few minutes finding a place in the lean-to for his saddle and bedroll before leading his grey back through town until he found the livery stable where he paid Jackson the owner, for a couple of days. Then he walked back along Main Street to the bath-house, paid his thirty cents, and soaked in a hot tub, feeling the grime of the trail oozing away as the steam rose about him.

The air of Main Street felt sharp against his face after the atmosphere of the bath-house as he stepped out in a clean shirt and a fresh pair of pants, and he was thankful that the townsfolk now paid him little attention. A couple of men still stood at the door of the funeral parlour but he swung past them before they had chance to ask questions. He had other things on his mind. There'd be good honest red meat at the Widow Powell's but a couple of beers first would finally wash out the trail dust. Lannigan felt a glow of anticipation as he pushed through the batwing doors of the saloon.

Plainsville's saloon was typical of those he'd been in a thousand times. A few tables stood around with rough wooden chairs. Tall mirrors on both side walls had been placed to make the main drinking area look bigger than it was. A Pianola stood at the foot of a flight of stairs which Lannigan guessed led up to the rooms where the girls carried on their business. He thought maybe they stayed upstairs until later in the day for there were only men in the place.

The old-timers had all left and in front of the long bar to his left stood a dozen men, rangemen by the look of them, clustered either side of a youngish fellow who sported a fancy leather vest and silver slathered over his spurs. Lannigan crossed to the other end of the bar where a fat, cheerful-looking barman, wearing a white apron over dungarees, was wiping down the bar.

Lannigan nodded towards the pump. 'Beer, and have another one coming up fast.' He put a couple of coins down on the bar.

The barman's welcoming grin spread wider. 'Just off the trail, I guess?'

Without waiting for an answer he pulled down a tankard from a shelf behind him, and held it beneath the pump. Lannigan watched the beer gushing from the tap. When white froth was bubbling over the top of the tankard the barman put it down on the bar counter. Lannigan stood for a moment watching the beer still swirling in the glass then he raised the glass to his mouth and poured half the beer down his throat.

'Sure tastes good.'

He raised the glass again, savouring the beer as it flooded his mouth. As he did so, there was a whoop and a shout from along the bar.

'Hey, boys! Just look who we got here!'

Lannigan had a mouthful of beer and his eye on the second tankard, and it was a second or two before he realized that the shout concerned him. When he turned his head he saw that the young dude with the fancy spurs had moved along the bar towards him. The dude's

28

eyes were bright and Lannigan caught the sweet smell of beer as he spoke.

'Howdy, stranger. Saw you come into town. Some time since we'd a killing in Plainsville.'

Lannigan put down his empty tankard and picked up the full one, looking closely at its contents. 'If you say so.'

'Yeah, that's what I'm sayin'. Benson!' he called without turning away from Lannigan. 'Tell the stranger about the last killing we had.'

A rangeman with a pock-marked face spoke up. 'Some no good gunslinger from down south came up here makin' trouble for your pa, Mr Jimmy.'

'And what happened, Benson?'

'You shot him plumb dead, Mr Jimmy, when he drew on you.'

The young man grinned at Lannigan. 'That's what gunslingers get in this town, mister.' He eyed Lannigan's ivory-handled Peacemaker. 'You ain't a gunslinger, are you?'

Lannigan examined the glass side of his tankard. 'Sure ain't,' he said.

'I'm real glad about that.' The young man's smile broadened. 'Strange you found the city *hombre* close to town when we all keep passin' Beaver Creek.'

Lannigan took a sip of his beer. 'Just lucky, I guess.'

There was a snicker of laughter from the rangemen, and the smile disappeared from the young man's face. For a moment he stood still, his eyes on Lannigan, then he twisted around in the direction of the men behind him. The laughter died and they looked back at him, their faces expressionless.

'You ain't finished your beer over here, Mr Jimmy,' a rangeman called out. 'Don't want it getting warm.'

'Shut your mouth. I'm talkin' to the stranger.'

He turned on his heel back to Lannigan. 'We're havin' a conversation. Ain't that right, cowboy?'

'Yeah, sounds like it to me,' Lannigan said evenly.

The kid was obviously some kind of bossman. Liked to throw his weight around. But Lannigan had guessed something like this would happen when he came into the saloon. Rangemen were notorious for grabbing news about anything, anywhere, and a killing was hot news. The kid was mighty pushy, though, beer or no beer, and he was standing closer than Lannigan cared for. He took a step sideways along the bar.

'Any ideas who might have done it, cowboy?'

Hell, the young dude sure was persistent. Lannigan took another sip of his beer. 'I'm a stranger hereabouts. You'd know more about a killing 'round here, I guess.'

'And what the hell d'you mean by that?'

Lannigan put his beer down on the bar. 'Now take it easy, feller. I'm just in here for a coupla quiet beers.'

'No goddamned cowboy tells me to take it easy!'

The young man's face had turned white with anger, spittle flying from his

31

lips. Lannigan saw a tall rangeman step out from the line of men at the bar and take a couple of steps forward.

'Let it go, Mr Jimmy. It ain't important!'

'Kansas, goddamnit! I just told you I'm talkin' to this cowboy!'

'Mr Jimmy, he ain't no cowboy. This feller's name is Lannigan. I seen him before in Dodge.'

The young man's head turned, his eyes shifting backwards and forwards between the tall rangeman and Lannigan.

'So what's special about Mr Lannigan?' he sneered.

'I seen him when he got out of jail on a pardon. Coupla jail rats knifed a guard and took a school marm hostage. Lannigan killed 'em with his bare hands 'fore they could harm her.'

Lannigan put his glass on the bar. The fat barman's grin had vanished and his eyes shifted nervously between Lannigan and the rangemen lined up at the bar.

'You sure about that, Kansas?'

'I'm sure, Mr Jimmy.'

The young man studied Lannigan with careful eyes.

'You ain't one of these bushwhackers thinkin' to stop my pa doin' his rightful business in Plainsville?'

To hell with it. He'd come back later when everyone had either sobered up or left town. He put his empty glass down on the bar and nodded to the barman. 'The beer was fine. But seems a man can't get a quiet drink in this town.'

He stepped away from the bar and turned to find the young man had moved behind him, standing between him and his path out of the saloon.

'You ain't goin' . . . ' the young man began.

Lannigan hit him two inches above his gun belt, his fist driving into the young man's gut. He went down on the floor as if poleaxed but he was young and strong and the beer hadn't slowed him as it might have done. He rolled on to one hip, his hand going for his gun and Lannigan took a quick step forward to slam down a high boot-heel on to his wrist, pinning it to the sawdust-covered boards.

'Anybody reaches for a sidearm had sure better know what he's doin'' Lannigan said, as along the bar the rangemen shifted. They suddenly stood very still.

Lannigan looked down. 'Let's get this straight, young feller. What goes on in Plainsville ain't no business of mine. I'm ridin' through as soon as I can. You got that?'

'The only place you're gonna ride is to Boot Hill.'

'You're Bart Hermann's son, I guess. Time your pa taught you some manners,' Lannigan said. Shifting his weight further forward, he increased the pressure of his boot. 'You talk some sense or you ain't gonna be handlin' a fork for your chow, let alone a sidearm.'

'OK, OK!'

34

Lannigan looked along the line at the bar, searching for the tall rangeman who had recognized him. 'Kansas, you tell this young fool's pa I ain't got no argument with him.'

Kansas nodded. 'I'll tell him. Might not take much notice, though.'

Lannigan hesitated for a moment, then he shrugged. He lifted his boot, waiting until he was satisfied the fight had gone out of young Hermann. 'I'm walkin' outta here,' he said. 'Don't try anything that'll get you killed.'

He glanced up at the mirror on the wall opposite the bar, checking that he would be able to see behind him. Then he walked slowly towards the batwing doors, his spurs ringing on the boards as he cleared the area covered with sawdust. He pushed through the batwing doors out into the afternoon sun, bright after the shadows of the saloon. For a moment he thought of walking over to Hudson's office, then recalled that Henry had ridden out to Beaver Creek. Forget it, he told himself.

What was done was done, and there was no going back. At least he'd drunk his couple of beers. The chow at Widow Powell's was all he was interested in right now.

3

'I guess you kinda looked forward to that fresh meat, Mr Lannigan.'

'Sure did, Mr McParlen. Jerked meat's fine on the trail but it sure don't do much for the appetite,' he replied.

The man who had addressed him was the keen-eyed Irishman in city clothes who had introduced himself earlier in the evening. Over supper McParlen talked about Texas and Lannigan told the Irishman something of his own time spent there. Now Lannigan stood up from the table.

'I enjoyed our talk, Mr McParlen. Maybe you'll join me out back for a smoke?'

McParlen pushed back his chair. 'I'll be with you shortly,' he said. 'I've a letter to finish before I take the stage.'

Lannigan nodded, turning to Widow Powell who sat at the head of the table.

'The late Mr Powell sure must have eaten well, ma'am.'

'Like a horse, Mr Lannigan, God rest his soul. You'll find coffee on the stove.'

Lannigan followed McParlen from the room, turning into a short corridor as the Irishman went up the stairs to his room. He entered a small room at the back of the house, and from the dresser he took a cup and poured coffee from the metal pot which stood on the stove.

Carrying the cup, he pushed through the wire screen door on to the back porch. The weather was clear and he stepped down and walked over to where a tree grew at the end of the yard. Leaning against its trunk, he took a sip from the cup. The coffee tasted good, and the blue and white cup sure made a pleasant change from the tin cup he used on the trail.

He bent to put the cup on the ground, then stood up and fished out the line bag from beneath his shirt and rolled a smoke. In the clear sky to the north stars were beginning to show and he grinned to himself. He always used to say there was one for him to follow. Well, maybe there was. Until he'd got their letter he hadn't even known his kinfolk were still alive. He drew the smoke into his lungs, the tobacco tasting good, and he exhaled contentedly.

Then he felt the gun barrel press into his neck, its gunsight screwing hard into his flesh, and he stood very still. Even had he been wearing a sidearm he couldn't have reached for it. His roll-up dropped to the ground.

'Caught the tough feller off his guard, I guess. Start walkin', Lannigan.'

The voice in his ear was a rough whisper, and the sharp gunsight was shoved even harder into his flesh. Lannigan considered spinning around and trying to knock the gun away, but then rejected the notion. This was no rangeman behind him. He'd have heard a cowboy at twenty paces. Prodded by the gun he walked on to the open ground beyond the yard.

'Over to that cottonwood, Lannigan, and keep mighty quiet about it.'

The voice behind him was still a rough whisper even though they were now well clear of Widow Powell's clapboard. A horse thief he'd once known whispered like that after he'd been cut down alive from a rope. But he was dead, shot in a jail riot a year past.

The branches of the cottonwood were starkly outlined against the darkness of the grassland which stretched away to the distant hills. At the base of the tree Lannigan could make out half a dozen men, the pale orbs of their faces turned in his direction. What the hell had they got planned for him? Only ten minutes before he'd been with decent folk. Hell, Plainsville wasn't some frontier outpost run by mule-skinners and crazy men who traded whiskey and guns with the redman.

He was now close enough to make out the features of the men. There was no sign of Hermann's son. A couple might have been rangemen but four had the rat-like features of no-good drifters like those he'd served time with. Men you had to watch all the time if you were to stay alive. Hard-faced, sidearms tied low on their hips, they watched his approach through narrow eyes, the moon picking out their unshaven faces in sickly yellow. For the first time Lannigan felt a tug of fear. Rattlesnakes like these would as soon shoot a man in the back as look him in the eye. The gun at his back dug into him again.

'Keep walkin' Lannigan.'

He took another pace forward and the night exploded into blackness shot through with purple waves. Vomit rushed to his throat, and he pitched forward on to his knees, knowing he'd been pistol-whipped. Hands clutched at his outstretched arms, tearing his shirt, and rope burned his wrist. His spurs dragged along the ground as he was hauled to his feet, kicking and strug-gling. He bunched the knuckles of his free hand and lashed out, but there was no chance of breaking free. The combined weight of the men slammed him against the cottonwood, the gnarls of bark smashing into his chest. His other wrist was roped and he was dragged even harder against the tree while other hands pulled his head back and a foul rag was forced against his lips. He had a moment to snatch a breath before the rag was rammed into his mouth by fingers clamped around his jaw.

The rasping whisper came from behind him again. 'Gimme a blade, Jake.'

There was the hiss of a knife being withdrawn from soft leather. Then Lannigan felt steel prick his skin, and the night air brushed his back as his leather vest and woollen shirts were cut from him. Blackness clouded his mind and when it cleared he knew what he was about to face. He had a memory-flash of being paraded in Fort James with fifty other men to see a trooper flogged for stealing from an officer. The rise and fall of the whip, and the sounds of the man screaming after the first few strokes was something he knew he'd never forget.

His body felt like ice, despite the runnels of sweat he could feel on his face, and the flesh of his back quivered at the crack of a bullwhip in the air behind him. Again, the whispering voice was close to his ear.

'Mr Hermann don't rightly know if some crazy townsman hired you. And he don't care neither. You're gonna be a warnin' to 'em all.'

The whisper went away, and Lannigan heard someone noisily fill his lungs with air. He bit down on the rag, feeling the side of his mouth scrape against the rough surface of the cottonwood, and steadied his eyes for a moment on the star he'd been looking at earlier. Then he screwed them shut. A second later the whip cut into his back like a branding iron, and he fought for air, choking on the filthy rag. Despite the rope holding him to the tree, he writhed around in a futile attempt to escape the fall of the whip. Again and again the white hot pain seared his back. If the men behind him made any noise he was unable to hear them. He heard only the crack of the whip, and he knew without the rag choking off his yells of pain he'd be hollering for them to stop. Then when he'd long lost count of the times the whip had cut into his flesh he could stand the agony no longer and the night swam into blessed darkness.

★ ★ ★

'There you go, cowboy. One more day and you'll be back on your horse.'

The speaker, Doc Evans, was an elderly, sharpboned man, who turned away from Lannigan to replace small bottles and a cotton swab in a black leather bag. He snapped the bag shut and slipped his arms into the jacket of his brown broadcloth suit, covering for a moment the gold chain of an Albert

44

which graced his ancient silk vest. As Lannigan pulled on his shirt and rebuckled his belt, Evans crossed the room to the pitcher standing on a washstand and poured water into a basin. He stooped over to scrub vigorously at his hands.

'Reckon there'll be scars you take to the grave, Mr Lannigan,' he said. 'But I've seen plenty of men with more.'

Lannigan buttoned his shirt, trying to ignore the stabs of pain which skittered across his back. He knew he'd been in this room of Widow Powell's for three days, but that's about all he did know, aside from the fact that McParlen, stepping out of the boarding-house for his smoke, had come looking for him. Lannigan had been told that both Doc Evans and Henry Hudson had seen him on that first night but he remembered nothing.

'Can't stop progress, I s'pose,' Evans said, as he dried his hands. 'But the railroad's sure bringing trouble to this town. Nothing'll stop Bart Hermann now Sheriff Hudson's gone . . . '

Lannigan jumped as if stung.

'What the hell d'you mean?'

Startled, Evans looked up from his hands. 'Don't get the wrong idea, son. Sheriff's heart gave out,' he said. 'Died in his office yesterday morning. Took thirty minutes to pass on.' Evans smiled grimly. 'Tough old bastard was giving orders to me and Charley Ford almost until his last breath.'

He threw down the towel on the washstand and buttoned his shirt cuffs. 'We'll need a new sheriff and real fast. Old Henry kept the lid on this town for the last coupla years, an' always finished a job he started. But Charley Ford's too old, and he's a mite too friendly with the Bar-T crowd for lots of folk's likin'.'

Evans took out of his bag a small leather pouch which Lannigan recognized as being an old Army dispatch case.

' 'Fore I forget,' he said. 'Sheriff had me get this from his room back of the

46

jail. Said you were to have it.'

Lannigan frowned. 'What's in there?'

'Old Army papers, I guess. But Henry was mighty keen for you to have them.' Evans chuckled. 'Said he'd come back and haunt us if we looked inside.'

He handed the buckled pouch to Lannigan. 'You know your lettering, son? Just in case there's something important?'

Lannigan grinned at Evans's expression of concern. 'My ma was a schoolmarm in the old country. Readin' and writin' was 'bout the only thing my pa didn't larrup me for.'

'Then I'll take five dollars from you for the visits. Don't do any hard ridin' for a few days.' He took the coins Lannigan handed him and slipped them into a pocket of his jacket. 'I s'pose you will be ridin' on?'

'Damned right, Doc, soon as I can. I ain't found this town too friendly.'

'Yeah, maybe you're right.' Evans opened his mouth as if to say something else. Then he appeared to think better of it, and twitched his shoulders in a shrug. 'I'll see myself out.'

After Evans had left and he was alone in the room Lannigan crossed to the window to stare in the direction of Main Street. Was it only four days since he'd ridden into Plainsville? Seemed a damned sight longer. He'd sure made a mistake in that saloon. OK, Hermann's son had set out to rile him. Stupid kid was going to get himself killed one day. But crossing a Hermann, even if it was the son, on his first day in town was plumb foolish. Hell, who would have given a damn had he walked out of that saloon earlier and away from trouble? Hadn't Henry warned him that tempers were boiling up around these parts? Trouble was, he hadn't listened to Henry. He'd been thinking too much of beer and chow and riding north. In a town like Plainsville he should have guessed he'd be a target when folk were beginning to choose sides.

But he sure would like to settle the

score with those who'd whipped him. Then he swore softly to himself. What the hell was he thinking, and what would settling some damn score prove? Hermann would still be running his spread and he'd maybe find himself railroaded back into jail or at the end of a rope. Best to ride north as soon as he could. He'd been dealt a low hand and he'd have to play it. But he knew he'd always have bad memories about this town. Asides from the whipping he'd missed taking a final whiskey with the man who'd twice saved his life at Wilderness, and that stuck in his craw.

Lannigan turned from the window and picked up the pouch from the table. The leather strap beneath the buckle was as thin as paper, as if Henry had opened and closed the pouch many times over the years. He pulled back the flap and saw the familiar Army insignia showing at the top of folded papers stained with dirt and sweat. They sure weren't much to show for a man's life. He upended the pouch, spilling the papers into a heap. Pushing them around on the table, he stared down at them, curious to know what he was supposed to do. He knew his old sergeant had no kinfolk. Perhaps Henry wanted the papers handed over to his own young kinfolk. Somehow keep Henry's name alive for a while. But the papers seemed ordinary stuff, nothing that youngsters would set any store by. Most of them were about Henry's time as Plainsville's sheriff. Another recorded his discharge from the Cavalry.

Now that was damned strange. Lannigan carefully read the next paper he'd taken from the small pile. It too was stamped with the Cavalry insignia but instead of mentioning Hudson's name it recorded the discharge from the Cavalry of a Frank Robert Lisher. What was Henry doing with this? He pushed the paper aside and picked up the next one, less stained and creased than the others.

'I'll be damned!' he said aloud.

Lannigan read the paper again to check that he'd fully understood the details. Satisfied he'd identified the paper correctly he let it fall to the table. Was this the reason Henry had sent him the leather pouch?

A knock sounded at his door. 'Mr Lannigan! You a decent feller in there?' a voice called.

'Come on in, ma'am!'

Lannigan stood up from the table as the door opened and he saw Widow Powell standing in the doorway.

'Thought you were still under them blankets, Mr Lannigan!'

'I want to thank you for giving me shelter these last three days, ma'am.'

Widow Powell tightened her lips. 'Bart Hermann was once a good friend of mine, Mr Lannigan. But seems now he's actin' plumb crazy. Maybe poor Mr Powell'd be with us now if we hadn't been forced to sell our old place.' She brushed her face with a strong hand as if to wipe away unhappy memories. 'Now you're up, there's eggs and biscuits from this mornin' if you can handle 'em,' she said.

'Sounds a mighty fine idea, ma'am. You mind if I ask you a couple of things? You ever heard of a Frank Lisher around these parts?'

Lannigan realized the extent of Widow Powell's surprise when she broke her own rules and took a couple of paces into his room. He saw her hesitate, her eyes examining his face.

'You ain't sassing me again are you?'

'No, ma'am. I ain't sassing you.'

'Lisher was my name 'fore I married Mr Powell. Frank Lisher's my cousin. Disappeared from Plainsville a coupla years ago. Only kinfolk I got if he's still alive, save my two boys down in Cheyenne.'

'Ma'am, I got some papers here from Henry Hudson. I reckon Henry might have got 'em from that dead feller I brought in. One of them's a land claim for a homestead. It says that Frank Robert Lisher owns two hundred and fifty acres centred on Beaver Creek. I know that's land Hermann uses for grazin' his beef.'

'But that dead feller you brought in wasn't Frank,' Widow Powell exclaimed. 'What d'you mean by all this?'

'I ain't rightly sure. But a couple minutes and I'll be down for those eggs and biscuits. Then I reckon we'll have a talk.'

When Widow Powell had closed the door Lannigan again crossed the room to gaze through the window in the direction of Main Street. He could just see the empty wooden chair in front of the sheriff's office. Doc Evans seemed to think that now Henry had gone Plainsville was going to fall into the hands of the Bar-T. When it had come to a showdown he knew Henry would have taken on the Bar-T even if it meant him standing alone. Evans had been right, Henry always finished a job he started. But if Henry had known his time was up maybe he'd made one last effort to have the job finished in the only way left to him.

Was this the meaning of the army pouch? Was his old sergeant now calling from the grave for Lannigan to go against the Bar-T? He knew that without Henry Hudson alongside him at the right time his own life would have finished when he was barely more than a kid. And saving the trouble he'd had down in Dodge, the years since the War had been good ones. Even if taking on the Bar-T meant him risking his life, maybe getting himself killed, he knew he couldn't turn his back on Henry. His old sergeant was calling in his debts like a man was entitled to.

As Henry lay dying he must have been willing to wager that Lannigan would settle those debts and try to finish the job that he no longer could. Lannigan looked at the Peacemaker in his gunbelt hanging from a hook on the wall. If he was going to reach his kinfolk before winter he'd have to get moving.

4

Lannigan made his way along the Main Street boardwalk aware that the towns-folk were eyeing him with curiosity. It was just as Widow Powell had forecast. When he'd agreed to help her with the Lisher claim she'd given him a warning. You have to remember, Mr Lannigan, she'd said, the men who established Plainsville are mostly dead. Nowadays the citizens can struggle more with their accounts books than they can with those no-good varmints out at the Bar-T. They see a feller like you in town and they get a mite uneasy.

A woman wearing a dark-red dress and carrying a broad-brimmed hat drew level with him. Thinking she was about to speak, he raised his hand to bid her good day, but she averted her eyes and passed without speaking. A few yards further on a man in city clothes turned on his heel and hurriedly crossed the street.

To hell with it, the sooner he finished his business here, the sooner he'd be riding north to his kinfolk. What were these townsfolk thinking? Did they think he'd ride out to the Bar-T, guns blazing like some damnfool in a Buntline dime novel? He sure as hell wouldn't be doing anything like that. Hudson's words came back to him from when they'd first encountered Johnny Reb. We'll pick off the outriders, Studs, he'd said. Then we'll hit the main body, and kill the officers first. The rest'll fall away.

'Mr Lannigan! Mr Lannigan, sir! Over here!'

Lannigan turned to look across Main Street at a short fair-haired man in a city suit who had his hand raised in greeting.

'I've something important, Mr Lannigan,' the man called.

Lannigan stepped down from the boardwalk and crossed the street. The fair-haired man greeted him with an outstretched hand which Lannigan shook.

'Thomas Cranmer, Mr Lannigan. If you'll step inside there's some legal business to attend to.'

Curious, Lannigan entered Cranmer's office. Two wooden cabinets were placed against a side wall alongside a large iron safe. Papers were pinned to a board on the far wall. A swivel chair stood behind a scarred desk, and on a thin carpet stood a high-backed chair which Lannigan guessed was meant for visitors.

'Sit down, Mr Lannigan. I'm not very fancy,' Cranmer explained, his voice giving the impression of nervousness.

Lannigan grinned, trying to put the lawyer at ease. 'I thought all lawyers were old and fat with silk vests.'

Cranmer shot a quick glance at him from pale eyes, then returned Lannigan's grin with a wry smile.

'That's Bart Hermann's lawyer down in Cheyenne you're talking about, Mr

Lannigan. Sure knows a lot about the law, though,' he added. He sat behind the desk and shuffled some papers before him.

'Sheriff Hudson left his affairs with me, Mr Lannigan,' Cranmer said. 'Frankly, the sheriff spent everything he earned, and maybe a mite more.'

'That sounds like Henry Hudson.'

The lawyer smiled briefly. 'But he did own a small clapboard near the schoolhouse,' he continued. 'Although the sheriff spent most of his time living at the back of the jail, so the clapboard's condition is unlikely to be good.'

'If it's any help to you, Mr Cranmer,' Lannigan said, 'as far as I know old Henry had no kinfolk.'

'That's correct, Mr Lannigan, and I suppose for that reason Sheriff Hudson left me to dispose of the clapboard.'

Cranmer squared his shoulders, giving Lannigan the impression that he'd reached a decision. 'I understand from Doc Evans that the sheriff passed to you his personal papers?'

Lannigan nodded. 'That's right.'

Cranmer smiled briefly. 'Then I'm confident that my decision is legally and morally sound. Mr Lannigan, the clapboard house is yours.'

Lannigan leaned back in the chair, taken completely by surprise. This sure was a new deck of cards. What the hell would he be doing with a clapboard house in Plainsville? By the time he'd finished the townspeople wouldn't give him spit on a rock. And it would come to that, he knew. He'd seen it happen before in Texas. Sure, he could sell the clapboard and take the money. But that would be like tossing it back into Henry's face.

'That's mighty generous of you, Mr Cranmer,' he said finally. 'But I don't aim to be here too long. How about if I use the clapboard until I leave town? Then you can turn it over to someone else. P'raps be useful to the school-marm.'

Cranmer beamed and he nodded vigorously in agreement. 'An excellent idea, Mr Lannigan. Henry always did have a soft spot for Lucy Walker.' Cranmer turned around a paper and pushed it across the desk in front of Lannigan. With a flourish he took up a pen, dipped the nib into an inkwell, and handed it across the desk.

'If you'd just make your mark there, Mr Lannigan.'

Lannigan took the pen, wrote swiftly alongside the place indicated by Cranmer's finger, and handed the pen back to the lawyer. Cranmer reached out and took the pen, looking down at the immaculate copperplate writing of Lannigan's signature. A red flush rose steadily from Cranmer's stiff white collar, staining his neck and climbing to his face.

'I hope you don't think . . . ' his voice trailed away, and his eyes shifted away from Lannigan's face.

'I ain't thinking anything Mr Cranmer, except that I was taking this to the bank.' Lannigan reached beneath his leather vest to take Hudson's pouch from inside his shirt. 'But I guess I'd be more than happy for you to hold it for me.'

'Yes, of course. Glad to be of assistance. In the strictest confidence, Mr Lannigan.'

His brief embarrassment overcome, Cranmer regained his calm manner, and reached for a broad stout envelope. He placed the pouch inside, and then sealed the envelope with red wax taken from a small box at the side of his desk. He picked up the pen again, glanced up at Lannigan and hesitated, then he wrote his signature alongside the wax seal. 'I'll keep this in my safe until you need it.'

Lannigan picked up his hat from his knee. 'One final question, Mr Cranmer. How long does a man have to work a homestead in this territory before he can claim ownership?'

'Five years, if I recall correctly,' Cranmer said. He smiled ruefully.

'There's not much call for homestead-ing law in these parts. But I'd be happy to check my lawbooks.'

'I'd appreciate that, Mr Cranmer.'

The two men agreed to meet at the sheriff's funeral the following morning, and Cranmer told Lannigan that the townsfolk had collected money for a headstone to be mounted on Hudson's grave.

'I'm not sure how we'll manage without your friend,' said Cranmer, as the two men parted company. 'He was all that stood between the town and the Bar-T.'

Lannigan recrossed Main Street, turning over in his mind the notion of owning the clapboard. The place solved one problem, that was for sure. Life was likely to get mighty rough over the next few weeks, and moving out would keep trouble away from Widow Powell. But he'd have to get some stores lined up. If he was going to shift for himself he'd want something fancier than the plain grub he carried on the trail.

He looked up to read the signboard and having made sure it was the store he needed he stepped up to the boardwalk and entered the General Stores. The early sun streaming through a side window cut through the shadows, and despite the time of day a couple of oil lamps hung above the counters glowed brightly. For a few seconds Lannigan stood a foot or so inside the doorway allowing his eyes to adjust to the change in light.

'Anybody around?' he called.

A tall gangly fellow in his early twenties appeared from a rear room and crossed the boards of the store to take his place behind the rough-hewn counter.

'Joe Martin at your service! Everything from coal oil to calico, cooking pots to candy!' In his clean dungarees the young man appeared almost to quiver with enthusiasm.

'Grandpa's over at a Town Council meeting, but I can get anything you want, Mr Lannigan.'

'Seems like everybody in town knows my name.'

'They sure do, Mr Lannigan. Everyone in Plainsville knows you're a famous gunfighter.'

Lannigan looked around the store before looking back at the young man and shaking his head. 'All the gunfighters are in the ground, Joe. And most of 'em deserve to be.' He nodded across the room past the pot-bellied stove to the right of where Joe was standing. The blue sheen of oiled gunmetal gleamed beneath the mahogany and glass of a cabinet fixed to the wooden wall. 'Mighty fine lookin' Winchesters you got there.'

'Best in the territory, Mr Lannigan. On account of . . . ' Joe broke off, his eyes dropping, and there was the sound of his feet shuffling behind the counter on the sawdust covered floor.

'On account of what?' Lannigan said, amused by Joe's embarrassment.

'Aw, well, I ain't meaning to boast, but I'm the champion Winchester shooter in these parts.'

'That sure must have knocked a few smiles off . . . '

Lannigan was interrupted by a woman's scream and the shrill whinnying of a horse from the street outside. He spun around and with a few strides was through the doorway of the store and on to the boardwalk. On the street in front of him a horse tethered between the shafts of a buggy reared high, eyes rolling, forelegs lashing at the air. In the buggy a red-haired young woman had been thrown almost on her back, her foot trapped, preventing her from being thrown to the ground.

'Hang on to those reins, ma'am!' Lannigan shouted.

He stood taut, knowing there was an even chance that the horse would plunge to the ground and stand there. But the animal slammed against the ground only to rear immediately again, the muscles of its hindquarters bunching and then rippling across its glossy skin. Lannigan vaulted the hitching rail and threw himself into the buggy, snatching the reins from the young woman. The horse, nostrils flaring and its breathing sharp and uneven, crashed once more to the ground, its oiled hooves kicking up the soil of the street.

'Hold tight, ma'am,' Lannigan shouted. 'He's gonna take off!' The horse leapt forward like forked lightning over the plains. The metal wheels of the buggy hissed through the soil of the street with Lannigan's warning shouts ringing out above the drumming of the animal's hooves as the buggy careered down Main Street past open-mouthed townsfolk. A cowboy ambling across the street looked as though he might jump for the horse's head. Then his leathery face showed doubt, and his chance was lost as the buggy shot past him.

Lannigan held the reins taut, half giving the spooked horse his head, half controlling him. As the buggy left Main Street and hit the uneven ground of the trail he braced his feet more firmly, gaining more room on the floor of the buggy now that the girl's foot was no longer trapped. Providing he could balance the buggy they'd be fine. But if the horse stumbled or shied, then the buggy would roll. It wouldn't be the first time he'd jumped clear from a wagon or rolled from a galloping horse. But the girl was unlikely to be so agile and would be badly injured, perhaps killed.

'We're doin' fine, ma'am,' he shouted. 'Just hold on!'

He shot a quick look at the girl who leaned away from him clinging to the side of the buggy, her face white, her eyes wide. As he suddenly realized that she hadn't made a sound, save for that first scream of shock outside the store, the pressure on his hands eased and he detected a change of pace in the horse's galloping hooves. With steady pressure he began to haul back on the reins.

'Easy now, feller,' he muttered, as the horse came out of the gallop, the pace slowing enough for the buggy to settle from its jerky progress to run evenly across the hard ground. Lannigan let the horse run on for another fifty yards before easing the reins further, until the horse was into a walk. Gently, he brought the buggy to a halt.

'Your foot OK, ma'am?' Lannigan asked, turning to the young woman who was sitting up, straightening the light shawl around her shoulders.

'Yes, thank you. Dollar's never done this before.'

The girl was trying to keep her voice even, but her face was still pale, save for thin red lines across her cheekbones, and he could see the shock still showing in her eyes. Lannigan recognized her as the girl who'd turned her head away when he'd brought in the body from Beaver Creek.

'I'm sure glad you hung on to those reins,' he said.

She nodded, her lips quivering slightly, as if for the moment she had exhausted her self-control. Lannigan looked away from her to the horse which now stood still, its flanks covered with white foam.

'Dollar sure looks lathered up,' he said. Without turning back to her he pointed across to a small creek a hundred yards from the trail. 'Why don't we walk him over there? He'll have a chance to gather himself before we head back for town.'

'Yes, I'd like that.'

Lannigan flicked the reins and drove the buggy across the springy grass. Halting beside the creek, he jumped out, and dropped to one knee beside the water. He scooped up water with his hat and lifted it to the horse, patting Dollar's neck and whispering softly while the horse drank noisily, his nose buried inside Lannigan's hat.

'Now that you've saved my life I should know your name.' He turned to look back at her and saw that the colour was coming back to her face. Her lips curved in a smile as she waited for his answer. He hesitated, then bent down and tore at the grass.

69

When he'd gained a couple of handfuls he stood beside Dollar, rubbing down his flanks.

'Don't rightly know about savin' your life, ma'am. But the name's Lannigan. Studs Lannigan,' he said finally.

He turned back to the girl who returned his gaze without a trace of shyness, and with no hint that she recognized his name. Sure has pretty green eyes, Lannigan decided. And she was tougher than she looked. Most of the womenfolk he'd known would be still shouting their heads off. And, he thought wryly, she must be the only one in Plainsville who didn't know his name.

'I'm pleased to meet you, Mr Lannigan. I'm Miss Hermann.' She hesitated fractionally. 'Miss Jane Hermann.'

For a moment his hand clutching the grass ceased its circular motion on the flanks of the horse. Then he moved again, continuing to wipe the sweat from Dollar. Mighty strange town

Plainsville was turning out to be, he decided.

'My name mean anything to you, Miss Hermann?'

Fine eyebrows above the green eyes drew together a fraction.

'No, Mr Lannigan, but it's not hard to guess you're a stranger. What brings you to Plainsville?'

'Happenstance, ma'am. I was ridin' north to take up some new work.'

'Something with horses, I imagine.'

'No, ma'am. Gonna oversee some drygoods stores for my kinfolk.'

Jane Hermann made a small choking noise, and Lannigan looked up quickly from Dollar. The girl was still gazing directly at him, but now her green eyes were sparkling with merriment, her lips tightly compressed. As their eyes met, her lips opened, showing white even teeth, and she laughed out aloud, her head tilted back, the sun catching the light on her hair. Maybe he'd been alone on the trail too long these last months but he reckoned Jane Hermann's laugh was the prettiest he'd ever heard. Like little silver bells he'd once heard when he was down in Texas. Only thing was, he couldn't decide what was so gosh-darned funny.

'Forgive me, Mr Lannigan. I'm forgetting my manners,' Jane Hermann said. She smiled at him again, a tiny dimple showing on her right cheek. 'But I just don't see you in a drygoods store.'

He finished scrubbing down Dollar's flanks, and dropped the handful of grass to the ground. Maybe Jane Hermann had a point. 'Sometimes I've trouble with it myself,' he admitted. He stepped back alongside the buggy and swung himself into the seat alongside her. 'Time we were gettin' Dollar back to town.'

On the drive back he learned from Jane Hermann that she'd spent five years back East, and that, Lannigan reckoned, explained a lot. Even the smart ladies he'd met when working in Texas carried the marks of living in tough cattle-rearing country. But Jane Hermann looked like one of those fancy ladies who had their pictures in books from back East he'd once looked through in a Kansas store. Her voice and manner sure were on the gentle side, and even he could see that her clothes were expensive, and the high-button boots which peeped from below her skirt probably cost more than he could earn in several months.

In answer to her questions about himself he gave vague replies, ducking away from anything which would admit to more than he wished. He turned the talk away from himself, content to listen to her voice knowing that she'd find out about him soon enough. When they reached Main Street he was again aware of the attention the townsfolk were paying him as he drove through the town. Seems as if a feller couldn't make a move in this town without somebody knowing his business. But it sure was a pleasure being alongside this pretty girl no matter if she did come from the Bar-T. As they drew level with the sign for Sam Bates, the undertaker, he halted Dollar and handed her the reins.

'Dollar should be fine now, Miss Hermann.'

'Thank you, Mr Lannigan, for everything.' Jane Hermann's lips curved into a full smile. 'Perhaps we'll meet again soon.'

He jumped down to the street and stood alongside the buggy, thinking to himself that he had never seen green eyes like Jane Hermann's in his whole life. 'Maybe we will, ma'am.' He touched the brim of his hat, then turned on his heel and walked away.

Sam Bates was setting fire to a cheroot when Lannigan entered the small room Bates used as an office.

'Howdy, Mr Lannigan,' the little man said, clouds of blue smoke circling above his head. 'You got a name for that feller you brought in from Beaver Creek? Had to bury him without a name. Hate doin' that to a man.'

'No, Mr Bates, I ain't.'

'Then I guess you're here about the sheriff. Henry's out back ready for tomorrow.'

Lannigan looked past Bates through an open door at the centre of the back wall. In the centre of the other room a pinewood box stood on trestles. Lannigan frowned.

'I heard the townsfolk had raised some cash.'

Bates nodded vigorously. 'They sure have. Been mighty generous. And every dollar spent honestly. Mason'll finish the stone by nightfall. Best one this town's seen for a long time.'

'I know about the stone,' Lannigan said. 'How much for the rest?'

Bates took the cheroot from his mouth. 'I ain't sure I follow you, Mr Lannigan.'

Lannigan pointed past him to the pinewood box. 'That ain't good enough for Henry. How much for your best casket? Your best wagon?'

A light gleamed in Bates's eyes.

'Finest wood I got for the casket. Smartest horses. Black plumes with crêpe. The best plantin' this town'll see for years. I can do it for twenty dollars.'

'Fix it, Mr Bates,' said Lannigan. He pulled back the points of his vest and brought out a handful of silver coins from the leather belt he wore beneath his gunbelt. He threw the coins on to the table in front of Bates.

'That'll take care of everything.'

'Sure will, Mr Lannigan!' Ash from Bates's cheroot spilled down his front as he quickly scooped up the coins and placed them in a pocket of his black broad-cloth jacket. He looked up at Lannigan.

'You like to see Henry? I ain't got him screwed down yet.'

Lannigan nodded. Bates led him into the back room, pushed his cheroot between his lips, and eased away the cover of the pinewood box, propping the long board against a nearby wall. Silently, both men looked down upon Hudson, dressed in a city suit, his magnificent moustaches smooth from their combing by Bates.

'Henry was a fine man,' Lannigan said.

'Sure was. Plainsville's gonna miss him.' Bates sighed. 'The town's gonna explode without old Henry keepin' the place in line. Hard to imagine he was here with me only an hour before he died. Brought across that Irish feller from Widow Powell's.'

Lannigan looked up at him sharply. 'You mean McParlen?'

'That's the feller. Irishman wanted to search the clothes of that dead 'un you brought in.' Bates shrugged and sucked on his cheroot. 'Don't know what he thought he'd find. Save for a few dollars the feller's pockets were empty. I'd already got his papers from a secret pocket in his boots.'

'Did McParlen find anything?'

'Don't see hows he could. But he went away with an Irish smile on his face.'

A few minutes later Lannigan stepped

out of the funeral parlour back into the sunshine of Main Street. How old had Henry been? Fifty-five maybe. Not a bad age for a man to die but he might have fancied taking things easy for a while after he took off his badge. Lannigan hesitated. Now he was close he'd a mind to take a look at Henry's clapboard. He'd go back to the General Stores later.

As he walked down Main Street he turned over in his mind what Sam Bates had told him. What had McParlen been figuring by taking a look at the dead man? He must have had some mighty strong reason for Henry to have brought him across to the funeral parlour. And just what had McParlen been doing in Plainsville, anyways? Even during their talk together McParlen had never said exactly. Lannigan kicked the side of the boardwalk, sending his spur ringing. There was something going on in this town that he hadn't yet got a handle on.

5

'Mighty fine sendin' off you gave old Henry,' said Doc Evans.

Lannigan and Evans were heading for a narrow alleyway which would take them back on to Main Street. Without answering immediately, Lannigan turned to look up the hill to where Sam Bates and a couple of men were outlined against the sky as they settled the headstone on Hudson's grave. His old sergeant had sure quit this world in style.

Doc Evans and Thomas Cranmer had stood either side of him while the black coach drawn by four horses had rolled up the hill towards them. He had watched impassively while four townsmen, prompted by Sam Bates, had lowered the mahogany casket into the ground, the morning light catching the brass handles. Around the grave the

79

townsfolk had fallen silent and some of the women had brushed away tears. Now, as he saw the knots of townsfolk breaking up to scatter to their homes and workplaces he felt better for knowing that other people would remember the name of Henry Hudson.

'Better I could've given Henry a few years sittin' around smokin' his pipe,' Lannigan said finally as he and Evans reached Main Street.

Evans grunted. 'Henry might not have been too keen on that notion.'

Lannigan managed a smile. 'Maybe you're right, Doc.'

He heard shouts from behind them, and looked back over Evans's shoulder. 'Now what's Ford getting all hogtied about?'

Together, the two men looked back at Ford, his hand waving in the air, behind a group of women heading towards them along the alleyway.

'Lannigan,' Ford shouted. 'I got somethin' to say.'

Evans took the Albert from his vest

pocket and glanced down at its face. 'I've a child to see, Mr Lannigan. I'll bid you good day.'

Lannigan stepped up to the board-walk, making room for the townsfolk who wished to cross the street. Several of the men nodded a greeting to him as he moved away, and a tall dark man called out. 'Mighty generous of you, Mr Lannigan.'

Ford turned the corner of the building and stepped up to the boardwalk, his face red.

'Thought you'd want to know straightaways,' Ford said. 'You can ride out of Plainsville, Lannigan. If Henry trusted you that's good enough for folks here.'

Lannigan stared hard at Ford, noting the clouded eyes in the flushed face. Ford sure looked like a man in the wrong business. If the town kept him on as sheriff, the Bar-T riders would be busting up Plainsville whenever they felt like letting off steam.

'I ain't ready to ride on yet,'

Lannigan said. 'Got some business of Henry's to clean up 'fore I leave.'

Ford frowned. 'Now what d'you mean by that?'

He waited for Lannigan to answer, his frown deepening as Lannigan remained silent, but then relaxed as he appeared to recall something.

'Yeah, sure. Guess you're talkin' about Henry's clapboard.'

Lannigan didn't reply directly. 'Anyways, I sure wouldn't want to leave town before the stage gets here tomorrow,' he said.

Ford's frown started to gather again. 'Why's that?'

'There's a package in the mail for the Town Council,' Lannigan said. 'Tells 'em all about that dead feller I brought in.'

'Now how the hell could you know that?'

'You recall the pouch Henry passed me? Paper in there telling all about it.'

Without giving Ford a chance to reply, he swung around and headed

down the boardwalk among the townsfolk making for their homes. He was
aware of the grim smile on his face.
Henry's body might be in the ground
but his voice was strong and clear in his
own mind. Pick off the outriders first,
Studs.

He strode out, shaking off the
sombre mood of seeing Henry laid to
rest. He decided to look in on young
Joe about the stores for his clapboard,
but he was still a few yards off the
General Stores when he heard his name
called from across the street. Sitting in
her buggy was Jane Hermann. As he
paused she waved in his direction.

Lannigan crossed the street and came
up to the buggy.

'Howdy, Miss Hermann.'

'Good day, Mr Lannigan. I'm sorry
you've lost a friend.'

'Are you, ma'am? Didn't see anyone
around from the Bar-T.'

She was still for a moment, her lips
pressed together, her green eyes intent
on examining his face. 'I know all about

you, Mr Lannigan.'

'You know what you've been told, Miss Hermann,' Lannigan said. He touched the brim of his hat. 'Good day to you.'

He turned on his heel and walked away from the buggy. To hell with her, green eyes and all. Soon there'd be a showdown with the Bar-T. Better he didn't start thinking about Jane Hermann with her fancy hats and her silk dresses.

'Mr Lannigan. Mr Lannigan! Please come back!'

For three or four yards he didn't break his stride. Then he remembered how she'd laughed yesterday when they were at the creek. Maybe he was wrong to start blaming her for what her father was doing. Hell, how many times in his life had a pretty girl, a real lady, called out to him like that? He turned and retraced his steps to the buggy.

She held a gloved hand to her chin in a gesture of regret.

'That was a foolish remark I made,

Mr Lannigan. I'm sorry.'

Lannigan shrugged, not too keen on knowing exactly which remark she meant. 'Guess I'm a mite troubled seein' Henry off.' He looked up briefly at the sky and then back to the girl who returned his smile. 'Too fine a day to fight, I guess,' he said.

Her face softened, and he knew he was going to remember those eyes for a long time. 'What brings you into town, Miss Hermann?'

'You do, Mr Lannigan.' Her face flooded with colour and she added quickly, 'I mean my father would like you to come out to the Bar-T and talk.'

'I thought you knew all about me,' he said wryly. 'There's no way I'm comin' out to your pa's ranch.'

'That's why I'm here. I'll take you in the buggy and bring you back. Pa's given his word.'

Now what the hell did she mean by that? Did she really think he'd hide behind her skirts? If Hermann wanted to see him then the rancher could ride into town. The first time he'd be out at the Bar-T would be with his Peacemaker when he called for the whispering coyote who'd had him flogged.

But hold on, maybe he was acting like a head-strong colt. Hermann was no backshooter if all he'd heard was true and if Hermann had given his word to his daughter, then he'd keep it. Besides, this could be a chance to see Hermann on his own territory, size up the man, see what he was going up against.

He stepped up into the buggy. 'Drive on, Miss Hermann. Sure is a day to be out and about.'

An hour later the buggy swung around a bend in the trail past a stand of cottonwoods. A quarter of a mile ahead the trail split, and as they drew closer Lannigan could see that the right hand fork led towards a track across which stood a high wooden arch. From the curved timbers of the arch, some twenty feet above the stomped down soil, a wooden signboard hung on chains, announcing the Bar-T. Knowing he was getting closer to home, Dollar quickened his pace, and the wheels of the buggy rattled over small stones as they passed beneath the arch.

A mile past the archway, the buggy breasted the top of an incline, and Lannigan caught his first sight of the Bar-T ranch house, solidly built from stone and wood. On either side, some distance from the main house, stood two long low buildings which Lannigan guessed were bunkhouses for the rangemen. As the buggy swayed along the track towards the ranch house Lannigan saw that behind the bunkhouse to the east was a large corral, and fifty yards beyond that a smaller one, its wooden fencing smartened up with a coat of whitewash. Save for an old rangeman cleaning some leather at the door of one of the bunkhouses, the place seemed deserted. But as Jane Hermann reined in Dollar to bring the buggy to a halt in front of the ranch house, a slim swarthy Mexican appeared through the open door and came down the steps to lead Dollar and the buggy away.

'Follow me, Mr Lannigan,' Jane Hermann said.

Inside the house she paused in the large open entrance hall and gestured towards the gunbelt which hung on a wooden peg beside the door. 'Do you mind?' she said. 'Father doesn't allow sidearms in the house.'

Lannigan nodded his agreement. He had no problems with that rule. Even had they been in a frontier town he wouldn't have felt comfortable walking into a man's home with a sidearm on his hip. He unbuckled his gunbelt and looped it over a second wooden peg. Jane Hermann turned and led him through to the rear of the ranch house along a corridor furnished with heavy mahogany furniture imported, Lannigan guessed, from back East, and maybe even from Europe. Above a gleaming four-legged mahogany server crossed sabres were pinned to the white-plastered wall.

At the end of the corridor Jane Hermann pulled open a heavy door on which metal fastenings gleamed, and Lannigan followed her into a large room which ran the whole length of the rear of the house. The room was dominated by a heavy oak table at the centre of which stood a huge silver candle-holder. In a high wooden chair at the head of the table, just beyond where the sun threw light through the large windows on to the polished wood, sat one of the biggest men Lannigan had ever seen. Bart Hermann, Lannigan guessed. Over two hundred and eighty pounds, Lannigan reckoned, and although Hermann was some years older than Henry had been, his face appeared to bear the flush of good health. From this range at least, Lannigan decided, Hermann looked formidable. Beside him sat Jimmy Hermann, looking down the room at Lannigan with surly eyes.

'Come on in, Lannigan,' Hermann boomed. 'Juanita! Coffee for Miss Jane and Mr Lannigan.'

From a side door stepped a Mexican girl, but it was the sudden movement behind Hermann which caught Lannigan's attention. From the shadows behind Hermann's chair, and into the sunlight, stepped a man Lannigan first thought was a preacher. Then, as the man bent to Hermann's ear to say something Lannigan couldn't catch, the rays of the sun caught the silk shirt and the fancy buttons on the silk vest beneath the long black jacket. Lannigan saw the break of the jacket an inch below his waist as he leaned forward. Hermann nodded in response to what was said, and the man stood to bow stiffly in the direction of Jane Hermann. Then he left the room by the door from which the Mexican girl had appeared carrying coffee.

Hermann gestured with a large hand at the chairs along the side of the table close by him.

'Forgive Mr Slade. He has work to do.' He turned to his son. 'And there is work waiting in the corral, Jimmy.'

'Aw, Pa! I reckon . . .'

Lannigan saw Hermann's face stiffen, and the young man hastily got to his feet. Without a backward glance at either his sister or at Lannigan, he walked across the room and out of the side door followed by the Mexican girl.

'I'll not take coffee, Father. I need to see Franco,' Jane Hermann said. 'He's looking at the buggy.' She paused and looked carefully at her father. 'Remember you gave me your word.'

Both Lannigan and Hermann were silent as she turned and swept from the room. When the door had closed behind her, and Lannigan had taken one of the chairs at the table, Hermann gave a deepchested coughing laugh.

'Seems you saved a strong-willed woman yesterday, Mr Lannigan.'

'Seems that way,' Lannigan said.

He eyed the big man carefully,

leaving the coffee before him untouched. What was going on here, and why was Hermann keen to talk? Sure, he'd maybe saved Jane Hermann from injury, and Hermann was grateful, but this was the man who'd had him flogged a few days ago. From what he'd heard Hermann had railroaded plenty of the townsfolk off their property or broken them with debts they couldn't meet. But now that he was closer to Hermann he could see red veins of weariness in his eyes. This was a man, Widow Powell had told him, who'd built up his own father's spread from a handful of beef and a couple of Mexican cowboys. Now folk said he was intent on taking over Plainsville before the railroad arrived. In that prison back in Kansas Lannigan had been forced to make quick judgements about a man, otherwise he wouldn't have lived too long. Despite the rancher's reputation, Hermann looked like an ageing bull having trouble controlling the herd.

'The way she hung on to those reins, Miss Hermann maybe could've handled Dollar herself,' he said.

'And maybe she could've got herself killed, Mr Lannigan. You made sure that she didn't.'

Hermann reached beneath the table and brought up a small leather bag. There was the clink of metal as he placed the bag on the table. 'Seems like you and my son had a few words, but that's past. Take it. The Hermanns pay their debts Mr Lannigan.'

Lannigan made no move to touch the leather bag. 'I ain't a man of means,' he said after a moment. 'But there's no way I'll take this.'

Hermann grunted as if he'd expected this answer from Lannigan. 'Then if I can't give you money, Mr Lannigan, I'll give you a chance to earn it. I don't mind telling you I like what I see. Come and work for me. I can always use a good man.'

So that was what this meeting was all about? Lannigan shook his head. 'I got other business on my mind than punchin' beef.'

In an instant Hermann's good humour vanished. He stared hard at Lannigan, his eyes hardening. For the first time since he'd entered the room, Lannigan could recognize the ruthless streak that ran through the old rancher.

'Then make sure that business ain't gonna cross my trail here in Plainsville.'

'We'll both have to see about that, Mr Hermann,' Lannigan said. 'Tell me, you got a hand workin' for you who ain't got much of a voice on him? Sounds as if he's been cut down from a hangin'?'

'Now what the hell d'you mean by that? You just met him,' Hermann said. 'Mr Slade ramrods around here for me.'

Lannigan pushed back his chair and got to his feet. He picked up his hat from a side table before turning back to stare down at Hermann.

'Then we're gonna run across each other, that's for sure.'

Hermann brought his large-knuckled

hand down on the table with a crash, causing cups to rattle and the silver candle-holder to jerk an inch across the polished wood.

'You threatenin' me in my own home, Lannigan?' Hermann heaved his bulk up from his chair, and the two men faced each other across the table. 'Maybe you got ideas of filling Sheriff Hudson's boots. Understand what I'm sayin', Lannigan? You try that, an' I'll have Slade bury you alongside him.'

Lannigan didn't move, staring back at Hermann, his face impassive. 'Widow Powell tells me you were once an honourable man.'

'Amy Powell's a fine woman!' shouted Hermann. 'You tryin' your damnedest to insult me?'

'Maybe you ain't running things around here any more. Maybe Slade's doin' things in your name you wouldn't want.'

Blood welled up in Hermann's face, blue veins throbbing on his temples, spittle flying from his lips. 'Get off the

Bar-T, Lannigan! 'Fore I break my word to my daughter!'

Hermann stepped back sending his chair crashing to the floor. He swung his bulk around and strode away from the table towards the side door, punching it open with a clenched fist before disappearing from Lannigan's view. Then the door was flung shut, the sound of its slamming sending echoes around the large room.

Lannigan smiled grimly. 'Sure struck gold there, Studs,' he said aloud.

He settled his hat low over his eyes, and made for the door. The short corridor was deserted as he made his way back through the house, and nobody appeared as he stood buckling on his gunbelt in the large entrance hall. He stepped through the open door of the ranch house but as the sunlight reached him he halted at the top of the steps. Thirty feet away, leaning with his back against a hitching rail, was Slade, looking up at him. Lannigan eyed him carefully, then went down the steps until he'd reached the distance from Slade that he favoured.

'Seems we meet again at a tricky time, Mr Lannigan,' Slade rasped. 'Folks giving their word an' all that.'

Lannigan felt tugs of pain skitter across his back. The rough rasp of Slade's whisper was unmistakable. This was the man who'd had him flogged.

'We'll meet again, Mr Slade. You can put money on it.'

'Then I'm sure glad it ain't now. You with a Peacemaker, an' me without a sidearm an' all.'

Slade pushed back his jacket to show Lannigan there was no gun at his hip. As he did so, a Mexican stablehand appeared from around the corner of the ranch house leading the buggy with Jane Hermann in the driving seat, the reins held loosely in her hand. The two men stood back from each other as the buggy halted, and Slade raised his wide-brimmed black hat.

He gave a slight bow. 'Miss Hermann,' he said. Then he walked away in the direction of one of the bunkhouses.

'I can get a horse from the barn an' leave it in town,' Lannigan said. 'I guess your pa ain't so keen on you drivin' me back.'

If Jane Hermann was disappointed by the outcome of the meeting between her father and Lannigan she gave little sign of it, other than to press her lips tightly together. 'No, Mr Lannigan,' she said. 'I made you a promise, and I need to see Lucy Walker about the school-room.'

Lannigan stepped into the buggy and took the reins from her. 'Then let me drive. Make sure Dollar's behavin' himself.'

They were both silent as the buggy drew away from the ranch house, Lannigan turning over in his mind his meeting with Hermann.

'Had you met Mr Slade before?' Jane Hermann said, breaking the silence as they passed the bunkhouse Slade was heading for. Lannigan wondered if there were men at the ranch who worked directly for Slade and who bunked down separately from Hermann's rangemen.

'First time I set eyes on him, ma'am. Why d'you ask?'

'I met Sheriff Hudson several times, he and Mr Slade, and you, Mr Lannigan, you're somehow alike,' she said. Then she smiled as if to dismiss her own thoughts. 'I'm probably talking nonsense.'

'No, ma'am,' Lannigan said slowly, 'I don't think you are.'

The buggy rattled over stones marking a path across the track leading to the two corrals some fifty yards away to their right. Lannigan pointed with the buggy whip towards the whitewashed posts of the smaller of the two.

'You usin' that for Dollar?'

'Yes, I ride every day. Back East I rode side-saddle. If I'm to be useful here I need to ride like a man.'

'You mean 'cross the horse?'

She nodded, and her cheeks turned

pink. 'Trouble is, the men come and watch me.'

Lannigan frowned. 'I don't see . . . ' Then he stopped and grinned. 'You mean you in pants, showin' your legs like a workin' woman?'

Jane Hermann's cheeks turned pinker. For a moment her green eyes, fixed on Lannigan's face, shone. Then she turned away to look at the distant meadows, and for a moment Lannigan thought she was mad at him. But when she turned back towards him, her eyes were still lit with amusement, and as the buggy rocked along the track heading for Plainsville the clear air of the open country rang with the sounds of their laughter.

6

Stars were fading and the rim of the sun was showing through the haze on the horizon when Lannigan, Winchester in hand, entered the livery stable. Inside, the powerful tang of horses came to his nostrils, and several of the animals shifted in their stalls, aware of his presence. In a corner a match rasped and an oil lamp flared, a man's face glowing in the yellow light.

''Morning, Mr Lannigan.' Jackson, the owner of the barn, limped towards him. 'Your grey's all saddled up. Been fed for a hard day's ridin'.'

Lannigan moved across to where his grey had been tethered outside the stall and held up his hand close to its muzzle. Blubbery lips rippled across his hand, then the grey took the biscuit that Lannigan had taken from Widow Powell's table.

101

He slid the Winchester into its scabbard and untied his grey. Horses whinnied and stamped as they passed down the barn and then Lannigan was out into the pale light of the early morning. The grey skittered across the ground at the end of its reins, smelling the fresh day, glad to be free of the livery stable. Lannigan swung up into the saddle, and rubbed the side of the horse's neck.

'Maybe a hard day for both of us,' he said aloud.

Once clear of the town Lannigan struck out to the south, careful not to give the grey its head. Given the chance he knew his horse would have galloped across the open grassland, but Lannigan held to a lope. If the day panned out as he expected, his grey would need all its strength.

Three hours' riding brought them to the birch trees south-west of the Bar-T which he'd seen on his buggy rides. There was little risk of being seen from the Bar-T but he was taking no chances. He tethered his grey to a tree and settled himself against a thick trunk, at the edge of the trees. Then he adjusted his spyglass to focus on the Bar-T.

'Sure hope we ain't wasting our time here,' he muttered to himself.

If his timing was right he reckoned to wait for a couple of hours before he saw any action. He trained his spyglass on to the bunkhouse he'd seen Slade enter the day before. If Slade's men were going to make a move he reckoned that's where they'd come from. He lowered the spyglass, drank from his water bottle, and pulled a twist of jerked meat from his pocket. He sure missed Widow Powell's eggs and biscuits.

Two hours later, as he was thinking that maybe he'd overplayed his hand, he saw three men emerge from the bunkhouse. Reaching for his spyglass he brought the three men into focus. Their swaggering walk and their side-arms tied low on their hips made it unlikely that they were rangemen. He kept his spyglass on them until they entered a barn and disappeared from view Then, after a few minutes, the three men reappeared, walking their horses. Lannigan watched as they mounted, kicked their horses into a gallop, and headed for the track running north from the ranch house.

Lannigan got to his feet, backing up between the trees to untie his grey and push his spyglass down into his saddle-bag. Then he swung up into the saddle, guided his grey through the stand of trees, and struck out at a gallop.

Using a fold in the open country to stay out of sight he rode westwards, breaking his grey's stride every two or three miles to check that the three riders remained within range of his spyglass. Once he thought he'd lost them when they dropped into an arroyo behind high ground. Then, a few minutes later, his eye straining at the spyglass, he saw them again with their heads down, riding hard across the open country. Ten minutes later he checked their progress again and smiled. As he'd anticipated, they were wheeling to the south-west.

No longer halting to check their progress, Lannigan headed for the high meadows to the south. On the high ground above the trail he reckoned to find cover from which he could watch the Bar-T riders. He was sure now that they were heading for the coach road well to the south of Plainsville, the only route the stagecoach could take into town.

An hour later, the flanks of his grey lathered with sweat, Lannigan was among cottonwoods thick enough to hide him and his horse. Below him he saw the three Bar-T riders reach the cover of thinly spread pines at the edge of a small creek. As he watched them one of the riders dismounted and moved across to climb a mound of grass, enabling him to look along the trail to the south.

Lannigan could see that as the trail bent between rising ground the Bar-T riders would remain hidden from anyone on board the stage. He was sure now they meant to steal the mail and that could be only because Ford had passed to the Bar-T Lannigan's news about the letter for the Town Council.

Lannigan stood up in his stirrups to peer above a branch and saw the stage, its dust cloud rising behind it on the trail. With the aid of his spyglass the clear air enabled him to see a red splash of material, probably a dress, worn by one of the passengers inside the coach. His fingers curled more tightly around the metal. There'd better be no damned heroes on the stage. Anybody got hurt and he'd feel as if he'd played the wrong hand. As the stage headed for the bend in the trail, he shoved the spyglass into his saddlebag and tautened his hold on the reins, bringing up the grey's head. Below him, he saw the lookout scramble down from the mound and race across to his horse.

Above the clattering of the stage-coach wheels, the cries of the stagedriver, urging on his horses, rang out across the open country. Lannigan could see him clearly now, a short man bulked out by his woollen coat, and alongside him a guard in a dark slicker, a shotgun resting easily across his knees. The stagecoach swayed as it took the bend, disappeared for a short while, then came into Lannigan's view again, rapidly drawing level with the pine trees which hid the Bar-T riders.

'I'm goddamned wrong,' Lannigan said softly. 'They ain't gonna take the stagecoach.'

But even as he spoke the Bar-T riders broke from the cover of the pine trees twenty yards behind the coach. All three now had bandannas pulled up over their faces, the leading rider with a rifle in his free hand, the two others with sidearms held high. Neither man on the stage looked back, the sounds of the three riders lost among the creaking of their swaying coach and the

107

thrumming hooves of their own horses. Lannigan saw the leading rider kick his horse into a faster gallop until he was keeping pace alongside the coach. Then with his reins held in one hand, he shoved his rifle through the door of the coach. Immediately, the other two riders fired into the air.

Aware at last that the stage was under attack, the guard swung around and blindly fired off his shotgun, but his aim was wide of the Bar-T riders. The higher crack of a sidearm rang out, and Lannigan saw the shotgun fall from the guard's grasp and go bouncing across the ground behind the stage while the guard clutched at his shoulder and fell back to his seat. With loud cries from the driver the horses were brought to a standstill, their flanks quivering, their snorting breath filling the air around them.

The rider alongside the stage kicked his horse to move up to the driver, shouting something which Lannigan couldn't catch, and the driver reached below his legs to throw down a bulky satchel. As soon as the satchel was hitched across the horn of the Bar-T rider's saddle, all three riders fired into the air. The stage jerked forward and within twenty yards the driver had the horses at a gallop.

Lannigan didn't wait to see more. He turned the head of his grey, cleared the cottonwoods, and headed back the way he'd ridden earlier. He'd have to change his plans. Sure, he now knew for himself that Charley Ford had been double-dealing but he hadn't reckoned on anyone getting killed. No longer could he just be a spectator. But he didn't fool himself that Slade's men would be easy to take. That trick stuff alongside the stage had taken a lot of riding. If the Bar-T rider handled a gun as well as he handled his pinto then he'd need to be watched.

His grey was beginning to tire but Lannigan urged him on, figuring that no matter which trail they took back to the Bar-T the three riders had to ride through the arroyo where he'd lost sight of them earlier in the day. That's where he'd take them, he decided, when they thought they were almost home.

Two hours later, at the edge of the arroyo, Lannigan slid from his saddle to the ground. His grey had tired badly in the last few miles and he knew that Slade's men were only minutes behind him. He looked around, choosing a spot twenty yards into the arroyo where the narrow track turned around the foot of a steep incline. He led his horse along the arroyo, then with one hand on the reins, the other pushing steadily at its flanks, he had the grey stand across the track.

Taking his hand from the horse's flanks, he shifted to press firmly against its shoulder, while pulling steadily on the reins. With his knee against the grey's leg he felt its weight rest against him for a moment, before he took a step back. Blowing air through dilated nostrils, the big horse sank to the ground. For a moment it kicked out, but then was still, its eyes rolling back, almost as if seeking approval for its cleverness. Lannigan pulled his Winchester from its scabbard, and threw himself to the ground behind the horse's body, levering the long gun before resting it across the fender of his saddle. Out of nowhere came a memory flash of the screams of Southern boys in their butternut brown as they fell under a Union ambush. He shook his head angrily, as if by doing so he would rid himself of bad memories. That all happened a long time ago, he told himself. No damn use thinking of things like that now.

'You ain't got long down here,' he muttered to the grey rubbing with his fingers at the horse's neck.

A few minutes passed and the throbbing rhythm of advancing horses came to his ears. Lannigan curled his finger around the trigger of the Winchester, his cupped hand steadying the barrel. Then the Bar-T riders swung into view. Shouted oaths cut the air as the three men saw the grey on the ground ahead of them. Lannigan pulled off two fast shots above their heads as he saw all three riders haul on their reins, pulling their horses' heads around in an effort to make for the higher ground.

'Back down on the trail!' Lannigan shouted.

One of the men reached for his holster, and Lannigan shifted his aim. As the man pulled up his gun Lannigan's slug struck him low on his shoulder throwing him back off his horse, and sending him rolling down the sloping ground back on to the trail. Lannigan levered the Winchester, sending brass spinning through the air.

'That's enough!' one of the men shouted.

Lannigan watched, as with their hands in the air, the two riders urged their horses back down on to the trail. He stood up slowly, his Winchester held in one hand, and took a pace clear of his horse. Keeping his rifle aimed ahead of him, his eyes on the two riders, he held the reins taut while the grey struggled to its feet. When the animal was standing quietly Lannigan let the reins drop.

'Unbuckle your gunbelts and let 'em fall,' he shouted.

'You're Lannigan, ain't you?' called the redshirted leader.

Lannigan tossed the Winchester across into his left hand, drew his Peacemaker and put a shot six inches above the speaker. White-faced, the man unbuckled his gunbelt and let it fall to the ground beside the other.

'Kick 'em away,' Lannigan ordered. While the men kicked out at their gunbelts, Lannigan swung up on to his grey.

'You in the red shirt! Bring over the mail satchel. An' move real slow.'

'I ain't aimin' to make trouble!'

The rider in the red shirt reached up to the horn of his saddle and unhooked the satchel. His eyes never left the barrel of the Peacemaker as he walked towards Lannigan. There was a click as Lannigan thumbed back the gunhammer, and the man put up a hand.

'Take it easy, Lannigan!'

Lannigan leaned down from his saddle towards the man and took the satchel. 'Now put that other skunk across his horse,' he ordered. He eased off the pressure on the gunhammer, and with one hand tied the satchel to his saddle while he watched the two men struggle to get the body of the Bar-T rider on to the horse.

'Now get on your horses,' Lannigan ordered. He pointed at the red shirt. 'You do the leadin'. You make a run for it, I'll shoot your horse from under you. If the fall don't kill you, I'll put a bullet in your neck.'

'I done told you, Lannigan. We ain't aimin' to make trouble.'

'Then back up your horses. We're goin' into town.'

His Peacemaker held loosely down by his side, he watched the Bar-T riders turn their horses. When the three horses were settled in a line he ordered them to move off and at little more than a walking pace all four horses headed back along the track. After a mile Lannigan turned them to the west and a couple of miles further on they regained the main trail leading into Plainsville. Lannigan didn't drop his guard but he judged the two men were not going to try anything. He just hoped he wouldn't run into any more of Slade's gunslingers.

Two hours later as he left the trail and reached the start of Main Street, the three horses of the Bar-T men a few yards ahead of him, Lannigan saw the crowd of townsfolk gathered around the stagecoach fifty yards beyond the saloon. He'd gone maybe another twenty yards when one of the townsfolk must have turned and seen him. A sea of faces turned in his direction and excited voices rang out from the crowd as men and women surged away from the stage and down Main Street towards him.

'Like the early days in Texas,' Lannigan muttered to himself, and shoved his rifle back into its scabbard. 'Up to the sheriff's office,' he called to the Bar-T riders.

By the time they reached there, Charley Ford was standing on the boardwalk, jail keys in hand, and he stepped down to take the mail satchel from Lannigan. Then three of the four horses were hitched to the rail by eager townsmen while Skinny gave Sam Bates a hand in leading away the horse carrying the dead Bar-T rider. Men and women called out, some of the men pushing forward to slap Lannigan's back, as he helped Ford get the two men through to the jail. When he was sure Ford had the men in separate cages he went out of the office on to the boardwalk. A crowd of townsfolk waited to hear the news. He started to speak but was interrupted as a cheer went up from the crowd, and questions were shouted to him.

'What happened, Lannigan? How

d'you get 'em, Lannigan?'

He shook his head. 'OK folks, show's over. Charley Ford'll tell you all about it soon enough.'

Ignoring the disappointed shouts he swung around and went back into the office, closing the door behind him. Ford was just coming through from the jailroom.

'Looks like mighty fine work, Lannigan,' he said. 'Stage shotgun'll be OK. Doc says only a fleshwound.'

'I'm glad to hear that,' Lannigan said. He stared hard at Ford. 'Now I ain't in the habit of listenin' to talk about a man. I like to find out for myself, 'specially in a town like this. So let's talk about your part in this hold-up.'

The deputy moved across to the desk and put down the bunch of keys, his eyes lowered, avoiding Lannigan's gaze.

'What the hell you gettin' at?' Ford asked finally.

'Why d'you reckon Slade's men robbed the stage?'

Ford seemed to relax a little. 'Obvious ain't it?' he said. 'They were after that letter to the Town Council about the feller you brung in from Beaver Creek.'

'There never was a letter, Deputy.'

Ford sank into the chair behind the desk. 'What the hell you talkin' about?' he said huskily.

'I set you up, Ford, an' you passed to the Bar-T what I told you. The stage shotgun been killed, it would've been down to you.'

'Now listen Lannigan . . . '

Ford's blustering was interrupted by the door swinging open and a short man swathed in a thick woollen coat entering the office. Lannigan took a moment to recognize him as the driver of the stagecoach.

'Howdy, friends,' the driver greeted them cheerfully, unaware of what had just been said. He glanced down at the mail satchel on Ford's desk. 'Sure am glad to see that again.'

He looked up at Lannigan and a

broad smile showed on his face. 'Mighty fine work, bringin' in those varmints. It's sure an honour to meet you, sir. Hasker's my name. You mind tellin' me yourn?'

'Lannigan. Studs Lannigan.'

The little man's smile grew even broader. 'Well, I'm goshdarned! Not only saved the mail for all the good people of this town but saved your own mail as well!'

Lannigan frowned. The cheerful driver must have got him confused with someone else. 'I ain't sure I follow that, Mr Hasker. Save for the folks around here there ain't a livin' soul who knows I'm in Plainsville.'

'That's as maybe. But an Irishman in Cheyenne gave me a packet for you. Handed me a couple dollars to make sure you got it.'

Now what the hell was all this about? Then Lannigan realized who Hasker might be talking about. 'Big feller? Name of McParlen?'

'That's him. Looks like a city gent.'

Hasker strode across to Ford's desk and rummaged through the mailbag. 'Here we are, Mr Lannigan. This is yourn sure enough!'

Lannigan took the package from Hasker and moved away from the two men. He tore off the cover and looked at the neat writing. He'd learned from their talk at Widow Powell's that McParlen was an educated man, and his hand showed it.

'Frank Robert Lisher died of a fever two months ago in Cheyenne,' Lannigan read. 'He worked for John Monroe whose body you found at Beaver Creek. Wild daisy in Monroe's slicker pocket.'

Lannigan looked up from the paper and stared unseeing across the office. Now what the hell was all this about? Why should McParlen take the trouble to send him this message? Sure, they'd enjoyed their talk in Widow Powell's and he'd been damned glad the Irishman had come looking for him that first night in Plainsville. But that didn't explain why he'd sent this package. Just who was McParlen, and what was his business in Plainsville? And what the hell was all this crazy stuff about a wild daisy?

7

Lannigan pushed away his plate. 'Guess I'll never cook biscuits as good as those, ma'am.'

'Folks say the Chinaman does a good breakfast,' Widow Powell said. 'How long you reckon on staying here?'

'Coupla days. I'll have Henry's place ready by then.' He sipped his coffee, turning his thoughts over before he spoke. 'You heard yet if Mr McParlen is comin' back?'

'Not a word so far.'

'You reckon he's a man to be trusted?'

'Mr McParlen struck me as an honest man. Didn't say much, save for that first night when you and he were talking. But he listened plenty, though. I sometimes thought . . . ' Her voice trailed away uncertainly.

'Thought what, ma'am?'

Widow Powell rose from the table. 'Maybe he's some sort of Government man from back East. Now I've got chores to finish.'

'Ma'am, I've got news of your cousin,' Lannigan said, putting down his cup.

She slowly lowered herself to the chair again, and looked steadily across at Lannigan, blinking rapidly several times before she spoke.

'Frank's dead, ain't he?'

'Yes, ma'am,' Lannigan said. 'Died of a fever a coupla months back.'

'Felt it in my bones,' Widow Powell said. 'Poor Frank. Never was the same after the War.'

'You maybe own a piece of the Bar-T ma'am, as Lisher's only kinfolk.'

'You still think that Homestead Certificate is genuine?'

Lannigan shrugged his shoulders. 'Don't see why not, but I'm told there's all sorts of law about home-steading. How long did Lisher work his place?'

Widow Powell didn't hesitate. 'Thirteen months,' she said firmly.

'You seem mighty sure about that, ma'am.'

'Frank started seven days after I laid poor Mr Powell to rest, and he left Plainsville twenty years to the day I brought my second boy into this world. I'll not forget those days in a hurry.'

'No, ma'am.' Lannigan was thoughtful. 'You know why your cousin left?'

'Driven off by those varmints from the Bar-T, I reckon.' Widow Powell's face darkened. 'I'm telling you, Bart Hermann's been set on the devil's work these last two years. The man's changed. He was good Christian folk 'til his poor wife passed on.'

'I ain't sure it is Hermann,' said Lannigan slowly. He stood up from the table. 'Anyways, guess it's time I looked at Henry's clapboard.'

'Your clapboard now, Mr Lannigan.'

He made his way across town amused by the changed attitudes of the townsfolk towards him. Folk who'd crossed Main Street to avoid him now seemed anxious to hail him. The young woman who'd turned away from him a few days before greeted him with a smile, flouncing the skirt of her dress with a gloved hand.

'Good morning to you, Mr Lannigan,' she trilled. 'Thank you for saving my brother's letter, and catching those terrible men.'

'Glad to help, ma'am,' Lannigan said, struggling to keep a grin off his face.

He found Hudson's clapboard back of the schoolroom fifty yards off Main Street. The voice of Lucy Walker, the schoolmarm, telling the children to open up their McGuffey's Readers, reached Lannigan through an open window. He was smiling faintly at old memories as he shoved at the weathered wood of the clapboard's door.

The rays of the early sun through the doorway threw his shadow on to rough floorboards as he crossed the room to the sagging wooden shutters. Then light flooded the room as they creaked open on hinges which hadn't seen oil for a long time, probably since a summer past, Lannigan reckoned. The stove in one corner of the room was dusty with old ash. To one side of the stove a bin was stacked with cordwood, and on the other stood an overstuffed armchair in front of a rough-hewn table and chair. The shade of the oil lamp hanging over the table, like the rough roof above, was blackened with soot. Lannigan shook his head in amused resignation.

'You sure didn't care for the easy life, old friend,' he muttered aloud.

Beyond the stove through an open door he could see a wooden cot covered with a palliasse from which discoloured straw was leaking. Lannigan crossed to a shelf on which stood a tin basin, and pulled back a dirty length of cloth. There had to be a bucket around somewhere. Then the door behind him banged loudly.

'Mr Lannigan!' Joe Martin stood frozen in the doorway, his rounded eyes staring at the Peacemaker in Lannigan's hand pointing directly at him.

'That was a damnfool move!' Lannigan slid his sidearm back into its holster.

'I didn't mean . . . ' Joe gulped. 'I've been lookin' for you.'

'So you found me!'

Lannigan looked around the room. Where the hell would Henry keep a bucket?

Had the old feller even owned a bucket?

'You gotta come quick, Mr Lannigan.'

Lannigan looked back over his shoulder. 'You got ants in your pants, Joe?'

'Sir, there's three Bar-T men just rode into town. Real ornery lookin' characters. And they've two spare horses!'

Lannigan looked at Joe squirming in the doorway, his face red with frustration. The three men weren't Hermann's doing, he was sure. The old rancher might not worry too much about his methods nowadays but busting men out of jail was risking trouble with the Union Pacific people. From what he'd heard, UP favoured a town being quiet before they brought in the railroad. But Slade would be playing a different deck of cards. Having two of his gunslingers shipped off to Cheyenne to break rocks for the rest of their lives could make his other men mighty restless.

'They're gonna break out those men from jail!' Joe exclaimed. 'Ain't you gonna do anythin' about it?'

Lannigan leaned against the edge of the table. He fished inside the top of his shirt for his linen bag, and sprinkled tobacco on to thin brown paper he took from a pocket in his leather vest.

'No,' he said, finishing his roll-up.

Joe's face grew bright red. 'Well, this is my town, Mr Lannigan! And I damn well am!'

Lannigan threw his roll-up down on the table, and covered the distance to the door in a couple of strides. He caught hold of Joe's shirt, swung him into the centre of the room, and shoved him down into the overstuffed arm-chair. Then he picked up his roll-up from the table, and set fire to it with a match.

'You ain't goin' nowhere,' he said.

As Joe pushed against the wide armrests and started to rise, Lannigan stuck out his boot and shoved him back down again.

'Listen to me, young feller. You go over there you maybe get yourself killed.'

'You brung those varmints in! You gonna stand back while they get sprung?'

'You get set on riskin' your life every day, and you ain't gonna live very long,' Lannigan said.

'But Plainsville's supposed to be law abidin'! We got decent people here tryin' to make a livin'! And Charley Ford'll get himself killed without help!'

Lannigan stared down at the young man's face, hot with anger and the need to do the right thing. Joe's heart was sure in the right place, he decided.

'Ford'll not get himself killed,' he said. 'Any sense he'll put down his gun.'

'Then he's goddammed yeller!'

'You watch your mouth, boy.' Lannigan said sharply. 'They ain't gonna be shootin' at carnival targets out there.'

Joe dropped his eyes in the face of Lannigan's anger, but jerked up his head suddenly at the sound of handguns being fired at the other end of town.

'How can you stand there, just smokin'?'

'Those gunslingers ain't goin' back to the Bar-T,' Lannigan said. 'Slade'll have told them to keep on ridin'. We got five for the price of two.'

'An' if Charley Ford gets hisself killed?'

'You ever wondered, boy, how the Bar-T knew so much about Henry Hudson's comin's and goin's?'

Lannigan walked across to pick up a bucket he'd finally spotted standing behind a wooden chest. Ignoring the confused expression on Joe's face he handed him the bucket.

'I'd welcome a hand,' he said. 'There's a well out back. I'm gonna fix that palliasse.'

An hour later Lannigan had the stove burning and drying out the damp timbers. He'd found a broom made of twigs lashed to a stout stick and had cleared the floor of the dirt which had built up for several months. The palliasse had been emptied of its straw and put aside to take to the Chinaman for washing. The tin mugs and plates had all been washed at the well. As Joe finally wiped a rag over the last corner of the floor Lannigan buckled his gunbelt around his waist again.

'Thanks for your help, Joe,' Lannigan said. 'Coupla days, an' this'll be fine.'

As he spoke, Joe stood up to look past him through the open doorway. Lannigan turned to see Doc Evans coming towards his clapboard. Joe came and stood alongside Lannigan at the door.

'I guess he ain't after me,' Joe said.

'Good day, Mr Lannigan.' Evans was grim-faced as he reached them. 'Those damn hold-up merchants got bust out. You hear the shootin'?'

'Sure did.'

'Charley Ford never stood a chance,' Evans said.

'Is he dead?' Joe asked.

'Lump on his head but he's fine. The shootin' you heard was those rough-necks scarin' off the townsfolk.'

'You send a posse after 'em?' Lannigan asked.

Evans shook his head. 'Ten years ago, Mr Lannigan, the whole town would've chased those roughnecks through hell-fire. Plainsville ain't got that sort of feller anymore.'

He took the Albert from his silk vest and glanced at the face. 'There's a meeting of the Town Council at eleven. We'd be mighty grateful if you were there.'

Lannigan's expression didn't change. How many days was it since he'd brought in Monroe's body from Beaver Creek? Six or seven? He knew Doc Evans was a good man, but he wouldn't be going to the meeting because Evans had asked him. Nor would he be going for the townsfolk. A couple days back they wouldn't have given him spit on a rock. No, he'd be going to the council meeting for what he owed Henry and to settle the score with Slade.

'I'll be there, providin' I can bring this here feller with me,' Lannigan said. He looked at Joe whose face was showing a wide smile. 'I'm gonna need somebody I can trust to watch my back.'

Joe Martin nodded his head vigorously.

'That'll be fine,' said Evans.

★ ★ ★

Shortly after eleven, in the big room at the back of the town's only hotel, Thomas Cranmer got to his feet to answer the question which had been

133

put to him by Evans. The lawyer looked at Lannigan and Joe seated alongside each other, then turned to the seven men who sat in the middle of the room on canewood chairs.

'You want Mr Lannigan running the law around here, then he has to be town marshal. There's no other way. Charley Ford can stay as deputy if he wants. But the town can't yet elect its sheriff.'

'So why don't we send to Cheyenne and get them to appoint a feller?' The speaker was a thin man with a long beard over the bib front of his dungarees.

'Because, Alfred, it'll take a month or more,' said a dark man who owned the barbershop and bathhouse. 'We ain't got that sort of time.'

'And Cheyenne'll send us a tax-collector when Plainsville needs a man who can handle a gun,' said a fat man in a city suit sporting a gold chain across his vest. 'The next gunslinger to come into town needs to be in jail mighty quick,' he went on. 'Plainsville's gettin' like a damn frontier town, an' I got a bank to run. We gotta do somethin'.'

'You suggestin', Mr Miller, we ride out to the Bar-T with guns in our fists?' Evans asked wryly.

The barbershop owner snorted. 'We'd probably finish up blowing our damn feet off.'

'We'll take a vote on it,' Evans said. 'Mr Lannigan wants four hundred dollars a month for being marshal.'

There was a sharp intake of breath from the men on the canewood chairs. Lannigan guessed they were remembering that Henry Hudson never got a dollar more than two hundred. It was Texas all over again.

'Doc, OK if I say somethin' 'fore the vote?'

Charley Ford was on his feet at the back of the room, a bandage showing below the rim of his hat. He looked across the heads of the men in the direction of Lannigan.

'Go ahead, Charley,' said Evans.

Ford turned his eyes away from Lannigan to look at the group of men in front of him. 'I been deputy 'fore this country 'round here was even a Territory. I always done my best, but . . . ' Ford hesitated for a moment then pushed on. 'Well, some things I done these past months I ain't too proud of, and I wanna chance to make up for 'em.'

Again he looked across to where Lannigan and Joe were sitting. 'You think Lannigan's askin' for a heap of money, but if he stays alive to collect it, he'll sure earn it. If he's gonna be marshal, I'd sure favour workin' for him.' Ford waited a few seconds then sat down again, his face set, staring ahead of him.

'Anybody else got anythin' to say?' Evans asked. 'No? Then let's vote on Mr Lannigan.'

Seven hands were raised and Evans turned to Lannigan.

'You got yourself a job, Marshal.'

Lannigan looked around the hotel

room, then across at Ford who was looking down at the floor. 'What's done is done, Charley. Glad to have you with me.'

He turned to face Jed Martin, Joe's grandfather, who sat in the centre of the councilmen, a frown on his face. 'When it comes to a showdown with those gunslingers from the Bar-T, Joe could be mighty useful.'

Jed Martin looked at his grandson. 'If this town's gonna go the way it should, then Joe has to play his part. An' he can sure shoot that Winchester.'

'I ain't seen him shoot yet,' Lannigan said. 'But I'm damned sure he'll stand and fight.'

'You goin' after those five gunslingers from the Bar-T?' asked Miller, the fat man from the bank.

Lannigan shook his head. 'They'll be headin' south. We'll not see 'em again.'

'But we know the Bar-T sent 'em into town! Hermann and this Slade feller are ridin' us into the dirt!'

'Supposin' I go out to the Bar-T, Mr

Miller?' Lannigan said. 'Hermann'll say he fired three no-good varmints for somethin' or other, an' who's to prove before a judge he's lyin'?'

'Then what about the stage hold-up? Those two busted out this morning were Bar-T riders! Hell, we even got a body up on Boot Hill.'

Lannigan shrugged. 'Same story.'

'The marshal's right, Mr Miller,' said Cranmer. 'Judge Warner'll have my hide if I bring him to Plainsville and waste his time.'

'Then I guess we're finished here,' Evans said.

Lannigan got to his feet as the councilmen began to move away. 'I'll see you in the office, Charley,' he called across.

He turned to Joe. 'You OK about all this?'

Joe looked up, his face set. 'Sure hope I can match those fine words of yourn, Marshal.'

'Nobody ever knows for certain, Joe, 'til the day he gets his chance,'

Lannigan said. He smiled encouragingly. 'We'll talk later.'

As Joe crossed the room to join his grandfather, Cranmer came to stand alongside Lannigan.

'I've been looking into that homestead business,' the lawyer said, when the others had left and they were alone in the room. 'Frank Lisher needed to work his place for five years to claim ownership.'

'Lisher's dead, Mr Cranmer, and he only worked his place for thirteen months.'

The lawyer frowned. 'One thing I've learned, Marshal, there's nothing ever final with the law. I'll go back to my books. There's always a chance I'll turn up something.'

8

'You need a horse mighty quick, Marshal, you take the big roan.'

In the livery stable, Jackson was rubbing down a stringy quarterhorse. As he scrubbed the fistful of straw across the animal's flanks, Jackson talked over his shoulder. 'Roan's the best horse I got here saving your grey,' he assured Lannigan. 'You gotta get ridin' some place and you can trust him.'

'You reckon new plates on my grey by noon?'

'Not a minute later, Marshal.'

Satisfied, Lannigan turned away from the liveryman to see Charley Ford appear at the entrance to the barn. There was something about the awkward way Ford moved that made Lannigan frown. He saw Ford hesitate as he screwed up his eyes to peer through the dust-laden air of the barn. Lannigan walked the length of the barn and both he and Ford stepped out into the open air.

'All quiet in town, Charley?'

'Bart Hermann's around. Wants to talk,' Ford said quietly.

'What the hell's bitin' you, Charley?'

Ford reached for the tail of his bandanna and mopped his face. 'That damned Hermann,' he said. 'Told me his lawyer'd make sure I ended up breaking rocks down in Cheyenne unless I did what he said.'

'What'd you tell him?'

Ford's eyes hardened. 'Told him p'raps he was right. Maybe I should be breaking rocks. And he could do his damnest 'cos he was getting nothin' more from me.'

'Where's Hermann now?'

'Seein' Miller at the bank.'

'Take another walk round town, Charley.'

He watched as Ford went off down the street. Seemed like nothing in

Plainsville was quite what it appeared, he decided. Henry must have guessed Ford had been tipping off the Bar-T with all they needed to know. He was too good a judge of men to be fooled for long. But had he been using Ford like a poker player in some game of double-bluff? Or had Henry let Ford keep his badge reckoning that one day he'd come right again? Calling a man's bluff when threatened with jail took a heap of courage from a man of Ford's age. Charley Ford, he reckoned, was beginning to get back his self-respect.

He took the side alley and followed the boardwalk along Main Street towards his office. Outside the bank two horses hitched to a wagon were tethered to the rail, and in the driver's seat was Kansas, the Bar-T man who'd recognized him from Dodge. Lannigan could see the shotgun straddling his knees. Maybe Kansas wasn't a range-man, after all. He crossed the street and came up alongside the wagon.

'Howdy, Kansas.'

'Howdy, Marshal, fine day.' Kansas looked at the badge on Lannigan's vest. 'Sure is a strange old world, ain't it?'

'What brings you to town, Kansas?'

'Doin' what I'm paid for. Ridin' shotgun for Mr Hermann, and that's all I do, Marshal. I sure hope you ain't puttin' me with those gunslingers working for Slade.'

'Then make sure you don't line up with 'em,' Lannigan said. 'Tell your boss I'll be in my office.'

Not waiting for a reply Lannigan turned and recrossed the street, his spurs jingling as he stepped up to the boardwalk. He stood aside and raised a finger to the brim of his hat as a fair-haired young woman carrying a wicker basket half full of eggs wished him good day. He entered his office and saw that Ford had already got a fire going, and he crossed the office to pour coffee into a tin cup from the jug on the pot-bellied stove.

He had set the cup by his elbow while rolling a smoke, and was trying to write with ink from a well which he reckoned Henry must have saved from the War when the door from the street opened. Lannigan looked up at Bart Hermann standing in the doorway, his huge bulk outlined by the light from the street. He put down his pen as Hermann came into the office to take the chair opposite Lannigan's desk, grunting as he lowered himself on to the hard wooden seat.

Hermann glanced briefly at the smoke between Lannigan's fingers before taking from his vest pocket a thin cheroot which he lit carefully with a wooden match. Apparently satisfied after a couple of deep draws he leaned forward towards Lannigan who, since the door had opened, had sat silent, his face giving nothing away.

'Reckon it's time you and me talked, Marshal.'

'What about?' Lannigan said. 'The five roughnecks been shootin' up the town?'

Hermann waved his cheroot in the

144

air. 'I ain't responsible for that. Slade fired all those five no-goods days ago. He found out they were runnin' off some of the stock, makin' money on the side.'

'The name John Monroe mean anythin'?'

If the sudden question Lannigan flung at him caused Hermann any concern then nothing showed on his face. He shrugged his massive shoulders. 'Lawyer of some sort down in Cheyenne, if I remember right. Wrote me saying he'd important business. Wouldn't talk to my own man. Said he was gonna come visitin'. But I never heard from him again.'

'How about your son? Could he have come across him?'

'If he had he'd have told me. Jimmy's a mite hotheaded but he knows better than to tangle in my business.'

'So Monroe never showed up at the Bar-T?'

'Marshal, I'm a wealthy man. I get crazy folks trying to reach me all the time. Monroe was likely another scam merchant with some damnfool idea of gettin' himself rich.'

Lannigan sent a cloud of blue smoke circling around his desk, leaving his roll-up in the corner of his mouth. He leaned back in his chair and folded his arms. 'You threatened my deputy a while back,' he said.

Angry red blotches suddenly appeared on Hermann's face.

'What the hell did you say?'

'Charley Ford's a sworn peace officer,' Lannigan said. 'Threatenin' him could land a man in jail.'

Worms of red blood appeared in Hermann's eyes and his whole face flushed vivid red. He leaned forward to grip the edge of the desk with thick calloused fingers.

'Are you out of your goddamn mind?' Hermann shouted, his eyes bulging with fury. 'I come in here for a friendly talk, Lannigan. Where the hell d'you think you are? You ain't back East or in some damn pilgrim town up north. This is cattle country, and that goddamn tin badge pinned to your shirt means nothing. In these parts the name of Hermann goes a long way, an' I can close down you and this hick town any day I'm minded!'

Lannigan didn't move, his face expressionless.

'I'm warnin' you, Lannigan . . . ' Hermann roared. Then he stopped suddenly, his mouth setting, as if he'd remembered something. Lannigan saw Hermann lift his shoulders in a gesture of resignation, and his anger seemed to disappear as quickly as it had shown, save for the red blotches which remained to stain his face. Hermann leaned his heavy body against the back of the chair.

'Oh, for crissakes, Marshal! Throw away that cowshit and take a decent smoke.'

He dug again into his vest pocket beneath his broadcloth jacket and pulled out another long cheroot, tossing it down on the desk. Lannigan glanced at the cheroot on his desk but didn't make a move towards it. He lifted his eyes back to where Hermann was blowing smoke towards the lamp which hung above the desk.

'What's the townsfolk payin' you, Lannigan?' Hermann asked. 'Two, three hundred a month? Four's gotta be their limit, I bet. That time you came out the Bar-T, I meant what I said. Come and work for me at the ranch. I'll make you a rich man, you have my word. Give me just five years and you do what the hell you like after that.'

'I ain't punched cattle since I was a kid before the War.'

Hermann pushed himself back in the chair, taking the cheroot from his mouth. 'Who the hell's talkin' about punchin' cattle? I can hire damn cowboys by the wagonload. I'm talkin' about ramrodding, Marshal. Keepin' a hundred men in line, makin' sure jobs get done when I want 'em done. Lookin' out for me an' my family when I ain't around.'

'You got Slade for that.'

Lannigan saw doubt flicker in the rancher's eyes. Maybe what he'd guessed at when he first saw Hermann wasn't far off the mark.

'You're damn right I have,' Hermann snapped back.

'Then you don't need me,' Lannigan said. 'Anyways, I don't work with the likes of Slade and his men.'

'Slade gets the men he needs.'

'They're no-good gunslingers, Mr Hermann, and you can't fight time with 'em. The country's changin' an' there's nothin' you can do about it. 'Fore long there'll be more Texas cattlemen comin' up the Santa Fe lookin' for grass. The UP's railroad means homesteaders comin' in, lots of 'em.'

'Slade'll fix them dirt farmers.'

'Slade's a rattlesnake. When he reckons the time's right he'll turn on you. He'll bring you down, you and all your family.'

Hermann jabbed a thumb across the desk. 'Slade's a hired hand! He does as he's damned well told!'

Lannigan stood up from behind his desk. He and Hermann could sit here until sundown trading hard words. But this meeting hadn't been a total waste of time. He knew it would take a damn sight more than a few words to divide the old rancher from Slade, but maybe he'd made a start. He watched silently as Hermann lumbered to his feet and headed for the door.

'I ain't got any problem with your rangemen. If they wanna let off steam on a Saturday night that's fine by me,' Lannigan said. 'Slade an' his gunnies come in, they're gonna end up in jail or worse.'

'I'm gonna tell you somethin', Lannigan.' Hermann's face was stained deep with his anger. His eyes glinted as hard as chips of rock, and his fingers opened and closed around the edge of the door.

'My old pa started the Bar-T with a coupla thousand acres an' a one-room hovel built of sticks and wattle. They carried him home wrapped in a wagon-sheet when I was just a young feller. I've been makin' sure the Bar-T's kept on gettin' bigger these past forty summers. An' one man with a gun an' a tin badge ain't gonna stop me now.'

Hermann stepped out on to the boardwalk slamming the door shut behind him. Lannigan stood, his eyes on the door as the noise bounced around the walls.

'You sure know how to quit a room, Hermann,' he said aloud to the empty office.

9

Lannigan unhitched his grey from the rail in front of the marshal's office and swung himself up into the saddle. He was looking forward to the day ahead of him. Sure, he needed to take a look at a couple of things, but it would be good to get out of town for a few hours.

'Any trouble, Charley, send Skinny lookin'. I'll be out at Beaver Creek, then up in those high meadows to the south-west.'

Ford was seated in the extra wooden chair which had been placed outside the marshal's office. From where he sat he could see the whole of Main Street. 'Any notion what time you'll be back?'

Lannigan shrugged. 'Before dusk, I guess.'

He touched his heels to his grey and made his way down Main Street. Some of the townsmen called out as he passed, and a couple of times he raised a hand to his hat to greet groups of townswomen. In front of the smithy a couple of Bar-T rangemen holding on to quarterhorses looked away as he drew level.

'Howdy, boys,' Lannigan called.

The two cowboys looked up, relief registering on their leathery faces. 'Howdy, Marshal, fine day,' the taller one said.

Once clear of Main Street Lannigan urged his grey into a lope, the animal snorting with pleasure as it felt the steady breeze on its coat. Likewise, Lannigan was at ease with himself in the morning sunshine. He'd need to keep his eyes peeled but that wouldn't stop him taking his pleasure from the day. Not so long back he thought he wouldn't be seeing open country for longer than he cared to ponder on. Three years, and he'd gone from lawman to chain-gang to lawman again. What had that Kansas feller said? Sure was a strange old world.

After an hour's riding he reached Beaver Creek pausing a while by the reeds as recent memories filled his mind. Then he slid from his saddle, and led his grey to the water. While his horse drank from the creek he sipped slowly at his water-bottle. Then he rolled himself a smoke and sat down on the grass, listening for a while to the waters as he drew on the tobacco. Later, a jack rabbit flashed away as Lannigan tossed the end of his smoke into the water and hauled himself to his feet.

He began to walk slowly along the edge of the creek, his head down, examining the ground. When he was fifty yards from his grey, he turned and walked slowly back, his eyes still lowered. For almost an hour he crossed and recrossed the ground, raising his head only once, then lowering it again to follow imaginary furrows between the water and the stand of birch. He'd reached the outer edge of the birch trees, and had decided to call off his search, when he heard a call.

'Mr Lannigan!'

He looked up in the direction of the voice. A couple of hundred yards away, Jane Hermann, astride Dollar, was standing in her stirrups waving a hand in his direction. Lannigan whistled his grey, his face creasing in a grin. Sure was turning out to be a good day. He swung himself up into his saddle, and walked the grey to where Jane Hermann had halted Dollar.

'Howdy, Miss Hermann.'

'I should call you Marshal now,' she said, glancing down at the badge on his chest, before raising her eyes to look straight into his. Jane Hermann sure was different to the unmarried ladies he'd met before who seemed to spend half their time looking down at the floor whenever a man spoke to them.

'I've been watching you for a little while,' she said. 'Are you surveying the Bar-T now?'

'Just lookin' for flowers, ma'am.'

Her delicate eyebrows lifted a fraction. 'You surprise me Marshal! And did you find any?'

'Not the one I wanted.' He leaned forward to stroke her horse's neck. 'Dollar's lookin' fine. How's the ridin'?'

She made a mock grimace. 'Dollar's going well. I'm not sure about the rider.'

'You mind if I tell you a coupla things?'

'Advise away, Marshal.'

'You were in my sights long before you called out. Around these parts you ride in on a feller, you tell him early. Or you're gonna get yourself shot.'

She looked at his face more intently, as if deciding whether he was making fun of her. Then her green eyes sharpened. 'I'll remember,' she said. 'What else?'

'Your ridin', ma'am.'

'What's wrong with my riding?'

'I ain't sayin' there's anythin' wrong. I guess that's the way you learned back East. But if you keep risin' out the

156

saddle like you're doin' then you're gonna get tired mighty quick. Fine for a few hours, but if you're gonna go ranchin' you could be ridin' for days.'

'I'm riding the only way I know. The rangemen are too busy to show me and you know about the others . . . ' she hesitated.

'I'm gonna have a look round up there,' he said pointing towards the high meadows. 'You wanna ride up there with me? Maybe I can help with Dollar. If you feel OK about that, I mean,' he added quickly.

When she answered he wasn't sure if she was making fun of him. 'I'm sure I'll be safe with a lawman,' she said. He pulled his grey's head away from where it was brushing Dollar's neck. 'Then let's ride, ma'am,' he said, kicking his heels into the flanks of his horse.

As the two of them rode alongside each other across country heading for the slopes of the hills Lannigan thought that had any rangemen been within earshot they'd have been mighty puzzled. His loud voice mingled with Jane Hermann's laughter as she attempted to follow his shouted advice. Then, after she'd held Dollar to a lope for several hundred yards only to lose it and uncomfortably bump up and down in the saddle, Lannigan, too, found himself laughing aloud as she threatened Dollar with being boiled for glue.

But by the time they reached the meadowland, a hundred-acre park with a blue-water lake, Jane Hermann was snugged down in her saddle, her heels thrust forward, and Dollar was moving across the ground at a regular pace.

'That's the way, ma'am,' Lannigan called. 'Guess old Dollar's gotten that lope in his blood, way he's carrying you along now.'

He reined in his grey, looking across the sea of grass and wild flowers, hearing mallards among the rushes at the lakeside. Sure was wonderful country, he thought. Jane Hermann brought Dollar alongside him, the exertion of the ride and her pleasure with Dollar's success had brought a glow to her face.

'Guess they've earned their water, ma'am. An' if you've a mind to take some coffee I'll get a fire goin'.'

They both dismounted and walked their horses to the edge of the lake, leading them along its edge until Lannigan was sure both animals could drink safely. In the clear water there were brown trout three times as long as a man's hand, and Lannigan spotted smaller speckled trout darting from the light into the shadows of the rocks.

'Sure wish I had a fishpole,' he said.

'At least you've found some flowers.' Jane Hermann was standing, hands on hips, gazing across at the swathes of wild daisies.

'Sure have, ma'am.'

Lannigan pointed across the meadow to where a large tree trunk lay on its side. 'Looks as if there's kindlin' wood over there by that trunk. Seems like some feller's been making camp up here.'

He turned back to the horses as they pulled their hooves from the soft ground, their thirsts quenched, looking for the fresh grass which grew at the top of the incline. Lannigan halted his grey with a hand on the cantle of his saddle, and from his saddle-bag took a couple of tin cups, his water-bottle, and a linen pouch containing coffee. Then he sent the animal skittering away up the slope with a slap on its hindquarters.

Dollar moved to follow the grey, and Lannigan bent quickly and put the coffee makings on to the ground before taking the animal's reins in his hand.

'You ever need to get away fast from a place with a hobbled horse, ma'am, you try this.'

He bent again and secured Dollar's reins to the animal's foreleg, then stood back, watching carefully as it moved away up the slope, the horse adjusting quickly to its hobble. He picked up the coffee makings and turned to surprise Jane Hermann studying him closely, a smile on her lips.

160

'Seems I've a lot to learn, Marshal.'

Lannigan shrugged. 'Guess most of us are learnin' all the time.'

They walked together across to the fallen tree, and while Jane Hermann sat on the trunk, Lannigan knelt by the ashes of the old camp fire. He worked swiftly and within a few minutes the kindling he'd taken up from beside the trunk was burning brightly. He fed the fire with larger pieces of wood, half filled the pot with water over coffee grains and settled it over the burning wood. For several minutes the two of them were silent, Jane Hermann breathing in deeply, her face turned towards the sun glistening on the blue of the lake. Lannigan watched the steam begin to rise from the coffee-pot. The Bar-T and Plainsville, he thought, sure seemed a long way away.

Jane Hermann broke the comfortable silence 'Have you thought what will happen when you meet your kinfolk, Marshal?'

'Some of the time, I guess,' he said.

She laughed. 'You'll probably find three unmarried young women keen to show you the town.'

'Five, ma'am, the letters from my cousin said.'

Her eyes widened, and for an instant her lips made a small circle. 'Oh!' she said, finally.

Lannigan got up from the fire, swishing the coffee around in the tin cups, and handed her one. 'Let that set an' it'll be OK. Though I guess it ain't what you're used to.'

'The coffee'll be fine,' she said.

Jane Hermann took the cup from his outstretched hand, her green eyes shining. He grinned back, wondering if she knew how beautiful she was.

'Guess you never drank coffee like this back East,' he said.

'Only ever from imported bone china and always with cream and sugar,' she said.

His grin broadened, knowing she was making fun of him, and not minding it a bit. 'How d'you spend your time back there?'

'Learning a little Italian, a little French. Riding English style. Playing the piano. I'm told I sing well.'

Lannigan took a sip of his coffee. 'That's mighty impressive,' he said slowly.

'But out these parts it ain't worth spit on a rock,' Jane Hermann said in a good imitation of Lannigan's speech. As he almost dropped his cup in surprise, she threw her head back and laughed. Then he laughed aloud too, the noise sending a little bird skimming from the branches of a tree close by, but then he saw her expression change, and her eyes grew dark with anxiety.

'Are you going to fight my father and Mr Slade?'

Lannigan hesitated. Jane Hermann was sure going to prove a handful to some man or other. Only a few moments before she'd been telling him that ladies like herself kept busy with things that didn't matter. Is this how womenfolk acted back East? Coming out with matters which concerned only the men? How the hell was he supposed to answer her?

'I ain't sure we have to talk about this, ma'am.'

'Don't treat me like a child, Marshal.' Jane Hermann's green eyes had sharpened. 'You've stepped into Sheriff Hudson's boots for reasons which I haven't really understood, but I do know he often clashed with my father. Now you seem intent on acting the same, and I'm worried about what might happen.'

'Then your pa shouldn't go hirin' a gunslinger like Slade,' Lannigan said.

'I think you're misjudging Mr Slade.'

'Slade's trouble,' Lannigan said. 'He's too fast pickin' up a whip to a man. An' I know he's a liar.'

'Nonsense! You've hardly spoken with him.'

Lannigan looked up from taking a sip of his coffee. The colour in Jane Hermann's face had risen again, but this time, he knew, from anger. Damnit, why did she have to ask these questions? Some women could have too many brains for their own good. But she'd started all this, and she was going to have to hear him out.

'You recall when I was out at the Bar-T? In front of the house Slade told me he was unarmed.'

'He was. I saw him walk down from the porch. You know father doesn't allow sidearms in the house.'

Lannigan took another sip of his coffee. 'Slade had a Derringer pistol in the fold of his coat. I saw it when he leaned forward to speak to your father.'

Jane Hermann hesitated. 'Are you sure?'

Lannigan didn't reply, sticking out a boot to nudge at the burning wood of the fire. She looked away from him in the direction of the lake where a pair of hooded-eyed fish-hawks wheeled across the water.

'You've worn a badge before,' she said finally.

He nodded. 'Town in Texas.'

'Tell me about it.'

Lannigan shrugged 'Not a lot to tell. A bad town needed cleaning up. I got elected.'

'And did you?' She hesitated over the words. 'Clean up the town?'

He nodded again. 'Yeah.'

'So why did you leave?'

'I got fired. Town got respectable, they didn't want me 'round the townsfolk. Me and my gun made them recall days they wanted to forget.'

'And now you're going north to run a store?'

'I stopped off in Dodge for a coupla years. But yeah, somethin' like that, ma'am.'

'With those girl cousins?'

'All five of 'em.'

She picked up her cup from the tree trunk, and stood up, tipping her cup upside down, spilling the last coffee dregs on to the ground. With a sudden jerk of his wrist Lannigan threw those from his own cup on to the ashes of the fire. Only leathery old working women should wear pants, he decided. Sure, times were changing, and there must be all sorts of crazy things happening back East, but real ladies unsettled a man by walking around showing their legs. One thing was for sure. If one of his cousins looked like Jane Hermann he'd sell his grey and run a store all day, no mistake. Then, as if determined to confirm all his suspicions about modern women, Jane Hermann said something which caused him to stiffen in amazement.

'Teach me to shoot your Peacemaker, Marshal.'

For the first time he realized how tall she was, her eyes level with his as he sat on the trunk of the tree. His hand dropped to the butt of his sidearm, and he shook his head.

'No ways, ma'am.'

'Why not?'

'The Peacemaker's a cannon. You ain't strong enough. Anyways, you shootin' a sidearm, well, it just ain't right.'

'Honestly, Marshal!' She thrust her hands on her hips, her legs braced. 'A six-shooter's not sacred!'

'I know it ain't ma'am. Just a tool of my trade, I guess.'

'The same trade as Mr Slade's?' she said. 'His gun is the same.'

He eased the Peacemaker on his hip. Doggone it. She was turning out sharper than Widow Powell. How the hell did he get himself into this barrel of tar?

'All the ladies back East as smart as you?'

'Only some,' she said, fine lines etching around the corner of her eyes. 'How do we start?'

He sat there for a few moments not moving. Then, steadily blowing air out of pursed lips, he pushed himself off the trunk and stood up. 'This ain't gonna work, ma'am, I'm tellin' you.'

Carrying his tin cup he walked ten yards across the grass and wild daisies of the meadow. Dropping on one knee he snatched at handfuls of grass and piled them into a mound, then placed the tin cup on the top. Getting back to his feet, he walked to where Jane Hermann was standing, her eyes bright with anticipation.

Lannigan slid his Peacemaker from its holster. 'First lesson you gotta learn is never to think a gun's loaded, and never think it ain't. Or you'll end up blowin' your foot off.'

Her eyes were as steady as when he'd warned her not to approach strangers without ample warning. 'I'll remember,' she said.

'An' never point the barrel at a friend, loaded or not.'

He swung away from her before bringing up the gun to the level of his gunbelt. His thumb pulled back the hammer.

'First you've to cock the weapon.'

He eased off the pressure, then moved behind her before handing her the Peacemaker. She took it from him, her hand dipping a little as the weight came on to her wrist. He waited until she was settled, the gun pointing towards the tin cup.

'OK, now pull back the hammer,' he said.

Her thumb went on to the hammer and she pressed down. The hammer remained still.

'Press harder,' Lannigan said.

'I am, damnit,' she said, her face screwed up with effort.

Lannigan reached forward and took the Peacemaker from her hand, slipping the sidearm back into its holster as he walked back to the fire. Ashes scattered over the brown-stained grass as he kicked out at the embers until he was sure the fire was no longer burning.

'Time we were gettin' back,' he said.

'No, wait! I've an idea!'

'No idea's gonna change a lady's hands.'

'Let me try again. Please, Marshal.'

He took one more look down at the fire and then turned, his mind made up that his Peacemaker was staying on his hip. Jane Hermann faced him on the other side of the fire, the front of her pale blue shirt rising and falling with excitement, her hands on her hips. He stepped over the grey ashes, came up to her, and gently turned her in the direction of the coffeepot on its mound. Then he slid out the Peacemaker and placed it in her hand. He sure as hell hoped he wasn't making a damned fool of himself.

'Forgivin' my words, Miss Hermann. But what the hell you doin' now?'

Jane Hermann had shifted her feet further apart to brace herself on the ground in a half-crouch. She held the Peacemaker high, level with her shoulders, her arms extended, her two hands grasped around the ivory-covered butt. The gunhammer was covered with her two thumbs. Lannigan heard a loud click as she cocked the gun.

'OK,' he conceded. 'But that's a crazy way to hold a gun. You'll never hit anything like that.'

'Try me,' she said breathlessly.

He moved slowly to stand behind her, sighting along the curve of her cheek and her raised arms. 'Squeeze the trigger, don't jerk it. An' watch the gun don't come back at you.'

Lannigan saw her arms grow more rigid, and her finger close slowly on the trigger. The Peacemaker roared and grass flew up ahead of them, a foot or so away from the tin cup.

Doggone. She maybe had something. He'd known cowboys who couldn't use a sidearm like that after trying for a month.

'Aim right and up a mite,' he said slowly.

His Peacemaker roared again. There was a clang and the coffee-cup went spinning away across the grass. Maybe he was lucky he hadn't really known a lady before. He reached for the Peacemaker, took a couple of slugs from his belt and reloaded before easing the sidearm back into its holster. When he looked up Jane Hermann had swung around, standing close to him, her face flushed, green eyes bright with triumph.

'That's two bits you owe me for the cup, Miss Hermann,' Lannigan said, trying to control his grin. 'I reckon we'd better be getting back.'

She ran for Dollar making whooping sounds and he settled the Peacemaker on his hip as he whistled for his grey while watching her. Sure was a crazy way for a lady to act. Maybe it was the red hair.

They rode down from the meadows back on to the flat land, heading back towards town and the Bar-T, not talking much, riding alongside each other at a lope. When they were about to part company at Beaver Creek Lannigan was of a mind to warn her again about Slade, but decided against it. He just hoped like hell she wouldn't get in the middle of trouble. He raised a hand to his hat as she turned Dollar away and headed for the hill and the track to the Bar-T. As she rode away from him he sat still in his saddle watching her. Then he was caught out when she turned to wave as if she'd known all the time that he was still there. He pulled at one of the grey's ears.

'Sure has been a day, old feller,' he said aloud.

He was a few hundred yards from Main Street when he heard the metallic clanging of a triangle ringing above the excited shouts of men. What the hell was going on? Kicking his heels into the grey's flanks, he thundered down Main Street. He was already half-way out of his saddle when he drew level with his deserted office. A townsman, carrying a heavy handpump along the boardwalk, his shirt blackened with sweat, hailed him from across the street.

'Sheriff Hudson's old clapboard,' he shouted. 'Burning like matchwood!'

10

In the early dusk the light from the yellow flames fell on the glint of fury in Lannigan's eyes. He stood taut, staring at the blaze, one hand resting on the ivory butt of his Peacemaker. He didn't need Sep Hardy, the town's blacksmith who doubled as firechief to tell him the clapboard was lost. The fire had already destroyed the main timbers, sending the roof crashing to the ground where it was burning fiercely among the embers of the floorboards. At the edge of the stinging belt of heat men ran around, some with blankets soaked in water, some carrying buckets, others wielding brooms to beat at sparks thrown out by the blazing fire.

Lannigan turned to look for Charley Ford over the heads of the crowd of men and women, their faces shining palely in the flickering light. Ford was fifty yards away, holding back a crowd of women and old-timers.

He walked over to Ford. 'Charley! You see any of Slade's men around?'

'Saw three ride into town just as the fire alarm went up. They were headin' for the saloon.'

'Go see if they're still there.'

'Right away, Marshal!'

Lannigan turned to the crowd who had grasped their chance to move closer to the fire. 'Any of you folks get closer, an' you'll spend the night in jail.'

Crazy folks'd get themselves burned if he let them. He turned his back on them and went back to the fire. The firefighters had abandoned the clapboard and switched their efforts to saving the buildings close by. Sep Hardy, his face streaming with sweat, left his men at the waterwagon and came across to Lannigan.

'We didn't stand a chance, Marshal,' he said. 'Fire took hold in minutes.'

'Any ideas what might have started it?' Lannigan's voice was harsh, and

Hardy looked at him carefully before answering.

'You got a broken kerosene lamp or anythin' like that?'

Lannigan shook his head. 'No damned kerosene at all.'

'There sure was a strong smell of kerosene, Marshal,' Hardy replied.

A townsman carrying a bucket who had heard their exchange as he hurried past, stopped and turned back to face Lannigan. 'You've been burned out, Marshal!' he shouted. 'Just like my pa!'

Lannigan swung away from Hardy as Charley Ford emerged from the flickering shadows and into the yellow light. 'You seen any of those rattlesnakes?' Lannigan asked.

'Three in the saloon. Playing poker,' Ford said. He tugged at his gunbelt. 'You want me to come across with you?'

Lannigan shook his head. 'I'll handle this. You're needed 'round here.'

Without waiting for an answer, Lannigan turned his back on the two men, and strode down the alleyway to Main Street.

Fifty yards along the deserted board-walk, his boots sounding loudly on the wood, took him to the saloon. He turned for a moment to look up Main Street, before slamming his hand against the batwing doors, setting them swinging behind him as he strode into the saloon. He saw that the bar area was deserted. Over to his right three men were seated at a table, cards in their hands. On the table before them were bottles and glasses and a pile of coins and bills.

All three wore sweat-stained hats and dirty leather vests over rough working shirts. Beneath the table Lannigan could see that the one in the centre, his legs pushed out from his chair, had the hilt of a knife protruding above the top of his boot. All three looked up from their cards as if aware for the first time that he was watching them.

Lannigan covered the distance to their table in four fast strides. With one wide swing of his left hand he sent bottles and glasses smashing against each other as they flew from the table. Coins spun through the air to bury themselves in the sawdust, cards and dollar bills fluttering down behind them.

Cursing loudly, the three men kicked over their chairs, and jumped back, their hands moving to the butts of their guns. Before two of the three men had touched their sidearms, Lannigan had drawn his Peacemaker, taken a pace forward and sideswiped the chin of the man to his right who had his six-gun half drawn. The man was sent crashing against his upturned chair before rolling to the floor and lying still.

The two others froze, their hands inches above the butts of their side-arms. 'Marshal, we ain't ... ' one started.

Lannigan shoved the table aside, took a further step forward and kicked the speaker an inch above the protruding knife hilt. There was a violent crack as Lannigan's boot drove into the man's knee and the man went down with a scream which he choked back in gurgles of agony.

'I ain't movin', Marshal,' the third man said quickly, his hands held away from his body.

'Drop your gunbelt,' Lannigan said, shifting closer to the two men on the floor. As the man unbuckled his belt and let it drop to the sawdust, Lannigan kicked away the half-drawn six-gun from the unconscious man. Bending quickly he drew the six-gun from the holster of the man clutching his knee and with a flick of his hand sent it skidding across the saloon. Then he backed away a few feet.

'S'pose you tell me your name,' Lannigan said to the man left standing. 'In case you got kinfolk who come around askin'.'

'The name's Wilson.' Beads of sweat had begun to glisten through the stubble of his unshaven face. 'What the hell d'you mean talkin' about my kinfolk?'

''Cause you're gonna be first, Wilson.'

Lannigan dropped his sidearm to hold it loosely down by his side, then he called out to the barman. 'George, you got any rope in that storeroom out back?'

'Yeah, I got some rope, Marshal.' George sounded hesitant, his voice hoarse. 'You sure you really want it?'

'Go get it, George, an' be damned quick!'

'Sure, Marshal,' George said and Lannigan heard him scuttle along behind the bar and open the door which led out back. 'What you gonna do?' Wilson's face, despite having turned ashen, was now covered in rivulets of sweat. 'We ain't done nothin'.'

Lannigan eyes were as hard as flint. 'I'm gonna hang you, Wilson, that's what I'm gonna do. An' after you, I'm gonna hang this here rattlesnake to stop him moanin'.' He glanced down at the still figure of the man he'd sideswiped with his Peacemaker. 'I reckon I'll just have to shoot this bastard first.'

Behind him there was a shout of protest. 'Marshal, you cain't do any o' that!'

'Shut your mouth, George, an' bring over the rope!'

George, as ashen-faced as Wilson, came from behind the bar, to hand the rope to Lannigan with a trembling hand.

'Marshal! I swear it! None of us burned you out!' The desperate plea came from the man on the floor, his two hands clutched around his knee.

'I ain't minded if you did or not,' Lannigan said. 'But I ain't wastin' time lookin' for the varmint that did. You three can take his place.'

'That ain't right, Marshal! An' you know it!' Wilson shouted, panic showing in his eyes.

'We ain't talkin' about what's right,'

Lannigan said. 'We're talkin' about a hangin' party.'

Wilson's eyes flickered to and fro as if seeking a way out of the saloon. 'S'posin' we told you who fired your place,' he said desperately.

Lannigan pulled back the hammer on his Peacemaker, and swung the barrel to point at the unconscious man on the floor. 'That ain't gonna save you. I get a name an' you ride back to Slade. I'll never see the sidewinder's hide.'

'Slade'd kill us if he knowed we'd told,' Wilson protested. 'We ain't goin' back to the Bar-T, Marshal. We give you a name an' we keep on ridin'.'

'Wilson's bein' straight,' groaned the man holding his knee. 'I'll take my chances with my horse.'

Lannigan gestured with his sidearm. 'How about this other skunk?'

'We take him with us,' Wilson said quickly. 'He ain't gonna be goin' back neither.'

Lannigan stared at Wilson for a few seconds, as if he was turning over in his mind whether to let the three go. 'You lie to me, an' I'll hunt you down. Then I'll make it a slow hangin'.'

Wilson's weak attempt at a smile showed he was beginning to hope. 'We know that, Marshal. We ain't gonna dangle at the end of rope for somethin' we ain't done.' He sucked in air through a mouth full of blackened teeth. 'Curly Harper's who you want.'

'How'll I know him?'

'Big dark sonovabitch. Knife scar on his jaw.'

Lannigan eased the hammer on his Peacemaker, and took a couple of steps back. 'Pick up this trail-trash an' get outta Plainsville 'fore I change my mind.'

'Sure, Marshal! We ain't gonna be trouble.'

A few minutes later Lannigan stood, Peacemaker in hand, as Wilson heaved up the moaning man still clutching his knee, and half carried him outside to his horse. While Wilson came back to struggle with the dead weight of the unconscious man on the floor Lannigan spilled the shells from the men's sidearms he'd recovered from among the sawdust. Then he followed Wilson as he staggered out of the saloon under the weight of the man across his shoulder. Flicking his head every few moments to throw off the sweat rolling down his face, Wilson roped the man across his saddle. Then he mounted his own horse to look fearfully down at Lannigan as he stepped forward. Lannigan shoved the three unloaded six-guns deep down into Wilson's saddlebag.

'You touch those before you're clear of Plainsville an' you'll join Harper's hangin' party.'

Wilson didn't reply, spurring his horse forward and Lannigan stood watching impassively until the three horses, one being led by Wilson, disappeared into the darkness. Lannigan knew he didn't have to think about them any more. Wilson and the other gunslinger had judged they were between a rock and a hard place. Either Slade would shoot them or Lannigan would hang them was the way they were thinking. They'd not stop riding until there was plenty of country between themselves and Plainsville. Lannigan swung on his heel and pushed back into the saloon.

'Gimme a whiskey, George,' he said, walking up to the bar.

George, his face still pale, took down a glass and a new bottle from the shelf behind him. Before placing the glass on the bar in front of Lannigan he wiped it with a clean cloth. He looked at Lannigan for a second, and then uncorked the bottle, tilting it to pour a generous measure of whiskey with a trembling hand.

'You was bluffin' there, Marshal. You know, playin' a poker hand? Just throwin' a fright into those varmints, I mean?'

George looked up from the bottle, confusion marking his fleshy face, as if he was suddenly unsure of what he was saying. Lannigan raised the glass and tossed off the whiskey, feeling the hot spirit running down his throat, warming his insides.

'I'll take another of those, George,' was all he said.

11

The following morning Charley Ford was using his fingers to count the score. 'That's eight of those gunslingers Slade's lost! This rate, Marshal, Slade'll be on his own in a couple weeks!'

'Don't fool yourself, Charley,' Lannigan said. 'We've just been hitting the outriders. We ain't even seen the main force.' He looked up suddenly as the door burst open. 'But it ain't gonna be too long, I reckon. What's the problem Joe?'

'Slade and eight of his men have just gone in the saloon,' Joe said excitedly. 'They sure look a mean bunch.'

Lannigan got to his feet, and crossed to the window. In front of the saloon a line of horses stood at the hitching rail.

'Open up that Winchester case, Charley. This is what we're gonna do.'

As the office came alive with the

harsh levering of the long guns, Lannigan told them what he wanted. Ten minutes later he pushed through the batwing doors of the saloon with Ford hard on his heels. Lannigan took in the scene. Lined up at the bar were Slade's gunslingers, flanking the black-suited figure of their boss. As Lannigan crossed the saloon and halted ten feet behind him, Slade glanced up at the mirror behind the bar, and turned around slowly. Lannigan saw then that Slade also wore his Peacemaker.

The rough voices along the bar were suddenly stilled, and one by one Slade's men turned around, their eyes settling on Lannigan who stood with his feet braced, thumbs tucked into his gunbelt. One of Slade's men, Lannigan saw, still held a beer glass in his hand.

'Get outta the firing line, George,' Lannigan called to the bartender and George shook himself and scuttled along the back of the bar.

'Howdy, Lannigan,' Slade said in his croaking whisper. He was leaning easily with his back against the bar, a thin smile on his face. 'Heard you had a fire last night.'

'Charley, take out your sidearm,' Lannigan said. 'You see the rattlesnake at the end with the knife scar on his chin?'

Ford drew his Colt. 'I see him, Marshal.'

'If he moves his hands, kill him.'

The gunslinger with the knife scar froze still. 'Now hold on . . . '

'Shut your goddamned mouth, Harper!' Slade rasped.

'You and your men are posted, Slade,' Lannigan said. 'Stay clear of Plainsville. You come in without a sidearm an' you'll end up in jail. You come in with a gun and I'll shoot you down.'

'I told you all to shut your goddamned mouths!' Slade croaked as muttering broke out along the bar. 'You ain't givin' me or my men any orders, Lannigan. Step outside and we'll finish this now.'

Lannigan stared back at him. Sure, why not? Shoot Slade down in the street and he'd be riding north by nightfall. Slade was the only one he need look out for. Kill Slade and his hired gunslingers would drop off like maggots. If this had been a frontier town he'd be waiting in the street already.

'The day'll come, Slade,' he said. 'But I ain't aimin' to turn Main Street into a shootin' gallery. The townsfolk want law not gunfightin'.' He let his hand rest on the butt of his Peacemaker. 'You all ride out, and stay out. That ways nobody gets killed. But Harper stays here. His burnin' days are over.'

'Boss, you said . . .'

'I ain't tellin' you again, Harper!' Slade croaked. His skin had stretched taut over his face, his eyes black slits against white. 'I give the order, we all draw. If Lannigan kills me, y'all kill him and Ford. You take from the Bar-T an' the town just anythin' you fancy.'

Slade pulled his lips back from his

teeth, giving him the appearance of a death's head. 'I got nine guns, Lannigan, you got yourself and an old man.'

'You ain't countin' me,' Joe Martin's voice came from the side of the saloon, as the barrel of his Winchester slid through the curtain to aim at the line of men.

For a second there was silence in the saloon. Then one of the Bar-T riders called out. 'I knowed that voice, boss. That kid'll be no trouble.'

The glass held by one of Slade's men exploded. A long furrow appeared on the bartop an instant before the slug buried itself into the wall with a loud thud. The ratchet noise of Joe's Winchester broke through the oaths of the men as they ducked away from the glass fragments spraying through the air. The man who'd held the glass stared down in shock at his bloody hand.

'Slade goes for his gun, Joe, leave him for me,' Lannigan called out. 'You take the men to his right. You know what to do Charley?'

Ford's voice was steady. 'Sure do, Marshal.'

Lannigan's fingers curled around his sidearm. 'Guess it's your call, Slade.'

Lannigan could see Slade struggling to control himself, the fury working behind his cheeks. Then Slade shook his head, moving his hand held well clear of his body. At a sign from Lannigan, Ford picked up the sack which he'd thrown on a table as he and Lannigan entered the saloon.

'Put your sidearms on the bar and step away,' Lannigan ordered. 'You'll get 'em back at the edge of town. No tricks an' everyone gets to see another day.'

'Do as he goddamn says,' croaked Slade.

Under Lannigan's steady gaze Slade and his men placed their sidearms behind them, Ford collecting them in the sack as he passed along the back of the bar. For the first time since entering the saloon Lannigan took out his sidearm, holding it loosely down by his side.

'And the Derringer,' he said.

Without a word Slade reached inside his coat and put the small pistol behind him. Charley moved back along the bar and slipped it into the sack. Then he came around the bar to stand alongside Lannigan.

'I'll take the sack,' Lannigan said. 'You take Harper over to the jail.' He thumbed back the hammer of his Peacemaker, but Harper stepped forward without a word and walked out of the saloon, head down, followed by Ford.

Lannigan eased back the hammer. 'You know what to do, Joe,' he called. The barrel of the long gun disappeared behind the curtain and a moment later the side door of the saloon slammed shut. At the same time Skinny's head appeared above the batwing doors.

'OK, Marshal. Your grey's on the rail.'

Lannigan took a couple of paces

back. 'You all mount up but don't move until I'm out there with you. Skinny's gonna be lookin' at you with a shotgun in his hands. Any tricks, Slade gets it first from me.'

As the men filed out of the bar, their eyes averted from Lannigan, Slade again leaned back against the bar.

'I shoulda known,' he whispered. 'A goddamned Yankee soldier-boy. I'm gonna enjoy killin' you.'

Lannigan stayed silent. Was it because of Slade's whisper that he hadn't guessed before that Slade was from the South? There was no mistaking the venom in his voice. Lannigan knew that it came from a hatred which went far beyond this encounter in Plainsville.

Then Skinny again called from outside. 'OK, Marshal.'

A few minutes later, under Lannigan's orders, the Bar-T men rode their horses down Main Street to the edge of town. Lannigan, with the sack of weapons looped over the horn of his saddle, brought up the rear, reins in his left hand, his Peacemaker held down by his right leg. Slade rode a few yards ahead of him. When they were fifty yards beyond the last clap-board, on to the rough ground of the trail leading out of town, Lannigan called a halt.

'You on the pinto. Over here,' he called to the last man of the group. Obediently, the pinto was turned and ridden back towards Lannigan who unhooked the sack and dropped it to the ground.

'Pick it up, and ride out. Joe Martin's in those trees behind you. You try and untie the sack and he'll kill you with his long gun. Slade'll be with you when you're out of gun range. You got all that?'

'I got it.'

Slade's man slipped off the pinto, picked up the sack, remounted, and kicked the animal ahead. By keeping Slade between himself and his men, Lannigan was able to watch the riders lope away while still watching Slade.

When he was satisfied that the Bar-T men were intent only on putting space between them and the town he shifted his attention back to Slade. Lannigan saw that his face was contorted with fury.

'Stay outta town, Slade. The townsfolk don't wanna see you around.'

'Two years! Two year's goddamned work!' Slade rasped. 'I'm gonna teach these goddamned store keepers and bible punchers a lesson they'll never forget!'

Lannigan felt the smooth ivory grip of his Peacemaker against the palm of his hand. He'd never shot down an unarmed man in his life and he wasn't about to start now. But there was only one way this was going to end. One of them was going to kill the other, and he reckoned that it would be soon. But he had made a promise to the townsfolk and he intended to keep it.

'Quit the Bar-T now Slade, an' we'll settle what's between us away from town,' he said. 'There's been enough killin' these past years. This town don't want more.'

'Then they were crazy to make you Marshal,' Slade croaked. 'You're dead meat, Lannigan. I'll see to that!'

'You'll get your chance,' Lannigan said. 'Now ride on.'

With a cruel kick at the flanks of his horse Slade sped away towards his men. Lannigan watched for several minutes. If he'd judged Slade rightly he'd lie low for a few days working out what to do and putting some fire back into his men's bellies. They'd make a lot of noise but they'd have no stomach for a fight if left to themselves. He knew he had to make plans. Once the few townsmen he could count on returned from the mine he'd get them together in case it came to a stand up fight.

He took a final look at the distant cloud of dust beginning to gather to the south of the town, and gave a long loud whistle. After a second or two, the figure of Joe Martin appeared from between the trees. Lannigan eyed him carefully as Joe covered the fifty yards between them. Joe had the Winchester firm in his grasp and his gait was steady, but his face was pale as he reached Lannigan.

'You did fine, Joe,' Lannigan said.

'Thanks, Marshal. Sure was different to what I expected.'

'You ever tasted whiskey, Joe?' Lannigan asked.

Joe shook his head and Lannigan grinned.

'Well, maybe your grandpa'll be after my hide, but I reckon you've earned some.'

Not waiting for Joe's answer he suddenly jerked up his head to look south. Above Joe's head a second smaller cloud of dust had appeared on the trail. He swung around to his saddlebag and pulled out his spyglass.

'They comin' back?' Joe asked, suddenly realizing what was going on. He spun around to face down the trail, dropping to one knee, and bringing up his Winchester.

'Hold on, Joe! Let's see what we got here.'

Lannigan brought the smaller dust cloud into focus and saw instantly what was creating it. 'Miss Hermann in her buggy,' he said. 'Slade's still heading for the Bar-T trail.'

Joe lowered his Winchester and got to his feet, the colour back in his face and smiling broadly. 'Guess I'm gonna have to wait a while longer 'fore I get to taste that whiskey.'

Lannigan looked down. 'Never knew a good rifleman who wasn't sassy,' he said deadpan. 'Get yourself some of those candy sticks an' put 'em down to me.'

He watched, amused, as Joe gave a mock salute, hoisted the long gun on to his shoulder and marched towards the town, his free arm swinging. Then Lannigan turned back to watch the buggy. Beyond Jane Hermann the dust cloud thrown up by Slade and his men had scattered in the breeze and the riders were out of sight over an incline. Lannigan sat easily on his grey, content to wait. Several minutes passed before Jane Hermann reached him. Then, as she brought Dollar to a halt close to his grey, he could see the worried look marking her face.

'Something bad has happened. I know it,' she said.

'Slade came in lookin' for trouble.'

She tautened the reins on Dollar, beginning to pull his head around. 'I'll have to get back.'

Lannigan nudged his grey forward and leaned over to take hold of Dollar's bridle. 'You'd be better in town.'

Her green eyes flashed. 'Mr Lannigan, you may be marshal of this town but that doesn't permit you to order me around!'

'I ain't orderin' you, Miss Hermann. I'm suggestin'.'

'I choose to ignore your suggestion,' she snapped, her face pink. 'Let go of Dollar!'

'I can't do that,' Lannigan said

slowly. 'There's no tellin' what Slade'll do now.'

'Slade'll not do anything. Father's about to get rid of him.'

Lannigan kept his face expressionless. He'd heard Henry's voice for an instant. Separate the officers and kill 'em, son. The rest'll fall away.

'That's when Slade'll be most dangerous,' he said. 'But I reckon your pa and brother'll be ready for that.'

The colour in Jane Hermann's face had faded away to be replaced by a worried frown. Yet her lips had tightened in a determined line, and her eyes had hardened. For a lady from back East she was certainly some woman, Lannigan decided. But he knew he wasn't going to let her go back to the Bar-T, no matter what she tried.

'I don't want you out there,' he said. 'Slade'll not care who he hurts.'

'That's all the more reason I should be with father and Jimmy.'

'They'll look after themselves.'

'But Slade wouldn't harm me!'

Lannigan felt his grip tighten on the bridle, causing Dollar to twitch against the hard knuckles grinding into the soft flesh of its head.

'Don't be so goddamned stupid! Those sidewinders are gonna be running wild out there! This ain't some lady's tea party back East!' He leaned over and jerked the reins out her hand. 'Now are you drivin' into town or do I carry you down Main Street like one of George's hurdy-gurdy girls?'

'Don't you dare touch me!'

'Then do as I'm tellin'!'

For a moment she sat taut looking back at him, her face marked with indecision. Then he saw her anger fade, her face once again marked with anxiety.

'But what will happen at the ranch?'

He kept his voice soft. 'Your pa and Jimmy'll be better off not havin' to worry about you.' Lannigan released his grip on Dollar's bridle and held out the reins so she could take them back from him. 'You spend a couple nights with

Lucy Walker an' times'll be back to normal,' he said.

'I pray that they will be, Marshal,' she said. She reached out for the reins, leaving her hand for a moment on top of his. Then with a flick at Dollar's back she drove the buggy away from him.

Lannigan watched her drive down Main Street before leaning forward to pat the neck of his grey. A short while back he was all ready for a gunfight in Main Street. Now all he could think of was Jane Hermann's slim shoulders moving away from him down the street, her red hair falling below the curve of her fancy hat. He blew out air between closed lips, and leaned forward again to tug at the twitching ear of his grey.

'Sure is a damned strange town,' he said aloud.

12

Lannigan waited while Thomas Cranmer pushed papers around his desk with a single finger. When he appeared satisfied that they were in order, the lawyer shuffled them into a neat pile before him.

'I've been taking a fresh look at homesteading law, Marshal,' Cranmer explained. 'You mentioned the other day Lisher spent only thirteen months out at Beaver Creek.'

Lannigan nodded. 'Widow Powell's certain of the time, an' I've had a look out there. But saving a few stones there's nothing left of Lisher's place.'

Cranmer frowned. 'That may not be a problem. But the law is clear. Five years of improving work are required before a land-parcel can be claimed.'

'Then I guess that means Lisher's kinfolk have no claim,' Lannigan said.

Cranmer pursed his lips. 'Not necessarily, Marshal. Homesteading law was intended to reward those who'd served the Union. Did Lisher spend any time in the Army?'

'Sure he did. With the Cavalry.'

Cranmer raised his right eyebrow a fraction. 'Any service in the Army may count towards those five years. We can check the period with the Army authorities.'

'Better than that, Mr Cranmer, look in that package I left you. Lisher's Cavalry papers are in there . . . '

Lannigan broke off as Cranmer, obviously startled, suddenly looked away from him to stare through the window overlooking the street. From outside came the sounds of a galloping horse charging down Main Street, and of a man shouting.

'That's Kansas from the Bar-T!' Cranmer exclaimed.

Lannigan jumped to his feet, and was out on the boardwalk in a few strides. His Peacemaker held high above his shoulder, he ran across the street to stand ten feet from where Kansas had reined in alongside a hitching post, his hands already held high in the air.

'Take it easy, Marshal! I ain't making trouble!'

Lannigan glanced at the sidearm on Kansas's hip. 'You know the rules, Kansas. Get down off your horse.'

'Fer crissakes, Marshal, I'm here to help!'

'That's as maybe,' Lannigan said. 'Just get down from your horse mighty easy.'

'Sure, Marshal, sure.'

Lannigan lowered his Peacemaker to his side as he watched Kansas dismount and stand by his horse. 'OK, both hands on your reins and walk your horse down to the rail outside my office.'

Without a word, Kansas slowly raised his free hand to the other already grasping his horse's reins. Then he turned and began to lead the animal down Main Street. Lannigan slipped his Peacemaker into its holster, and turned around to the small knot of townswomen who had gathered to watch.

'Nothing to worry about, folks. Go about your business.'

Charley Ford, his hand resting on the butt of his Colt, came out of the office to meet them as Kansas drew level with the hitching rail.

'OK, Charley,' Lannigan called. 'In the office, Kansas,' he ordered.

He watched while Kansas tethered his horse, and followed him up the steps to the boardwalk and into the office. He pointed at the chair in front of his desk.

'Now tell us what you're gettin' all fired up about.'

Kansas sat down, leaning forward in the chair as if by showing his determination he could convince him of the truth of what he was about to say.

'There's all hell breakin' out at the Bar-T,' he said.

Lannigan stiffened. 'Slade's turned on Hermann?'

'Damn right he has, Marshal.'

'Hermann and his son still alive?'

'Far as I know. They're holed up in part of the ranch house with some of their Mexicans.'

'How about Hermann's cowboys?'

'Bunkhouse been empty for four or five days. They're all out with the beef.'

Lannigan studied Kansas's face. He sure looked as if he was telling the truth. But that might mean only that Kansas was a damned good liar.

'So how d'you know Slade's turned renegade?'

'His men were talkin'. They know I ain't a range-man, an' they thought I'd join 'em.' Kansas looked at Lannigan, then at Ford, and then back to Lannigan. 'Slade's talkin' about hittin' this town like a prairie storm! You're gonna need help, Marshal. He's gotta pack of trigger-happy no-goods out there. Once Slade gets 'em liquored up they could burn out the whole town.'

'So why you worryin'? It ain't your town.'

'Fair question, Marshal.' Lannigan saw Kansas's eyes shift away. Either he was lying or he was getting his thoughts into some kind of order before he answered. Lannigan wasn't sure yet either way. Kansas turned back to face him, his face grim.

'I've had a gun in my hand for too long, Marshal, an' I ain't gettin' younger. I wanna stay in Plainsville. Throw in with you, an' I'll never need to pick up another gun.'

'If you're talkin' straight maybe we'll both be on Boot Hill,' Lannigan said.

Kansas nodded. 'I know it.'

Lannigan remained silent, weighing up the truth of what Kansas was telling him. What had Slade to gain by sending Kansas? Having his own man already in town was poor exchange for the advantage of a surprise attack. And what was Kansas supposed to do? Backshoot anyone defending the town? The notion made no sense, and anyways, Kansas wasn't a back-shooter, that was for sure.

'They any idea you rode into town?' Lannigan asked.

'Told 'em I wanted no part of shootin' 'round townsfolk an was ridin' west.' Kansas had visibly relaxed now that Lannigan had accepted his story. 'An' I told 'em they'd better be fast if they were gonna try an' stop me!'

'Any notion of when Slade's comin' in?'

'I reckon he'll be here before nightfall.'

'Goddamnit!' Ford exclaimed. 'All the fellers could have helped are over at the mine.'

Lannigan got to his feet. 'Charley, get hold of Skinny. Have him clear all the townsfolk off the street. An' tell 'em to stay off. Tell Skinny I want Sep Hardy with the longest length of rope he can find. Then I need Joe and Doc Evans across here as fast as they like.'

He swung around to Kansas again. 'Get hold of Jed Martin. Tell him I need all the ammo he's got in store. Winchester, forty-five, and shotgun. The town'll pay.'

'Right, Marshal.'

'One more question, Kansas. What brought Hermann to the bank a couple days ago?'

'We was movin' all the silver from the Bar-T . . . ' Kansas broke off, as he saw what Lannigan was getting at.

'Slade knows there's no pickin's left out at the Bar-T,' Lannigan said grimly. 'I'll bet he's gonna try for the bank first.'

Half an hour later Lannigan's office was crowded. Against the door leading to the jail stood Charley Ford and Kansas. Either side of the stove stood Skinny and Joe Martin. The blacksmith, Sep Hardy, in the far corner, towered over them all. In the chair in front of the desk sat Doc Evans. Lannigan was about to speak when the door opened and Thomas Cranmer and George from the saloon, joined the group.

'I can shoot a pistol, Marshal,' Cranmer said.

'I ain't sure what I can do,' said George. 'But there must be somethin'.'

'Glad to have you with us.'

Lannigan's face betrayed none of his thoughts. He knew that aside from himself and Kansas there wasn't a man before him who knew what they were up against. They maybe thought they did. The townsfolk never tired of talking about the old days when Plainsville saw a couple of killings every week and liquored-up cowboys shot at each other across Main Street. Sure the town had seen its share of trouble for the last couple of years but Henry Hudson had held the line. Today, Lannigan knew, Slade was intent on breaking that line. If Slade acted as he expected, he would aim to loot as much as he could before he and his gunslingers rode out, and if anyone got in their way they'd be shot down without mercy. He looked around the group, pausing at each man for a few seconds before moving on.

'They don't know we're waitin' for 'em,' he said. 'An' surprise is the best weapon. We'll cut 'em down before they're half-way down Main Street.'

He picked up the blackened piece of wood he'd taken from the stove, and drew several lines on the wall which the men faced.

'Joe and Kansas with long guns, high up. Joe on the saloon, Kansas on the roof of the drygoods store.' He made a couple of crosses on the wall. 'I'll be with Joe as they come in, then I'll get down to the street.'

He looked across to Ford. 'Charley, you and Skinny have your shotguns on the corner by the bank, here.' He made another cross on the wall. 'That way you don't risk gettin' caught in crossfire. An' Charley, try an' make sure nobody strays back on to Main Street thinkin' everything's over.'

'Where do you want me, Marshal?' Cranmer asked.

Lannigan looked across at the lawyer's determined face. If he put

214

Cranmer in the street the lawyer would be dead in less than a minute, and he guessed that Cranmer knew that before he walked through the door to offer his help. There were some mighty fine people in Plainsville, he decided.

'Down behind this desk with your pistol, and you don't move. We'll tie the door open, an' you shoot anyone who comes through aimin' to bust out Harper.'

'How about me?' Sep Hardy asked. 'I got enough rope in my place to tie up Texas.'

'I want you and George here together.' Lannigan chalked another cross on the wall. Then he explained what he needed from them, taking them through the details of his plan a couple of times.

'You both got that?' he said, when he'd finished.

'Got it, Marshal,' Hardy and George said together.

'OK, make sure you all have plenty of water with you. We could be in for a long day. Kansas'll sort you out with ammo. I'm gonna have a word with Doc Evans.'

Grim-faced, the men left the office to carry out the tasks they'd been given. Evans waited until they were both alone in the office.

'You want me close by, I guess.' he said.

Lannigan nodded. 'Me and Kansas, we're gonna have to take what comes. Any of the others get hit, I wanna give 'em a chance.'

'I could set up in the saloon,' Evans said. 'Amy Powell'd be useful. She nursed for me when we had the fever here a year or two back.'

'That'll be fine.' Lannigan looked out of the window watching Skinny as he moved along the boardwalk on the opposite side of the street. 'You know Doc, I sure ain't done this town any favours. Some fine men could get killed today.'

Evans stood up tugging at the points of his vest. 'Marshal, ever since Slade moved into the Bar-T somethin' like this was goin' to happen. Plainsville survives today, and we'll never look back. The town's damned lucky you're here.'

Evans got to his feet and crossed the room. He turned back to Lannigan as he opened the door. 'I reckon Henry Hudson would've said you're doin' OK.'

After Evans had closed the door and he was alone Lannigan stood staring through the window. 'I ain't that certain, Doc, but I could sure use you around here now, Henry,' he said aloud.

13

An hour later silence had descended on Plainsville. Skinny had done his job well, scurrying between homes and stores to warn the townsfolk of what was coming. At Skinny's urging the women had hastened to throw across the shutters in their homes, or to hurry down to the schoolroom if they first had to collect children. Only two old men, notorious for moaning and grizzling at each other, had given trouble. Ignoring Skinny's threats, they had refused to move from their clapboard at the back of the bank. Instead, they had taken down ancient muzzle loaders, telling Skinny they sure weren't quitting their home for a bunch of varmints from the Bar-T. Skinny had left them seated in two old chairs, their rusting long guns across their knees, arguing over fair shares of chewing-tobacco.

When Skinny had left him Lannigan had crossed the street to look into the saloon. Amy Powell, who had changed to a cheap cotton dress covered with a thin canvas apron, had been busy tearing up old linen for bandages. Doc Evans, wearing an old surgeon's coat, had raised a hand to Lannigan, but had been more intent on setting out his instruments.

Now Lannigan, with Joe alongside him on the balcony of the saloon, looked down on Main Street watching Ford and the rest of the men taking their positions. He saw George and Sep Hardy reach the corner of the board-walk near to the smithy and turn to look up towards him. Lannigan held up the red cloth in his hand and both men waved to show him they could see his signal.

Turning away from them to look further down Main Street, he realized that the others were already in position. He called out to each of them in turn, checking they could all hear him from their hidden positions across the street. Behind him, Joe was filling the gaps of the open balcony with thick planks of wood. As Kansas answered him, the last man he had called, Joe shouted behind him.

'Marshal! They're comin'!'

Lannigan swung around to look south. Joe was standing rigid, arm extended, pointing to where a cloud of dust was moving towards the town. Lannigan reached for his spyglass. By the size of the dustcloud, he reckoned there must be at least twenty men advancing on the town. As the cloud drew closer, the scene in his eyepiece cleared and he could see the riders moving forward in a tight formation.

'They sure are, boy,' he said slowly.

He'd never fooled himself that Slade was trailtrash like the rest of his men. Keeping those backshooters and liquor-crazy gunslingers under control meant he was both intelligent and ruthless. But what he could see in his spyglass meant that Slade was something more. Probably by threats and kicks, and maybe a shooting or two, he had welded his men into what looked like a disciplined force. These men weren't riding down on Plainsville just to kill him and a few townsfolk who got in their way. Slade knew he was finished at the Bar-T, and had offered his men other rich pickings. Slade was intent on sacking the town.

Watching the riders break from the Bar-T track and hit the main trail Lannigan had a memory flash of a Johnny Reb charge on his troop, his own officer dead, Henry on the ground, a Minié slug in his shoulder. Only by hand-to-hand fighting, stabbing and slashing, had some of them managed to come out alive after the two forces had clashed. This time he knew he had the advantage of surprise but if any of them were going to survive the bloody clash that was coming his plan had to work first time. There would be no second chances.

He could now see the oncoming riders clearly through his spyglass. Four galloping horses strained in the shafts of a low wagon, their backs lashed by a long whip in the hand of the driver, who half stood, legs braced, behind them. A few yards behind the wagon with Slade at their head, his black jacket cast aside for working shirt and vest, were two lines of riders. Each man, save for Slade, held his reins in one hand only, the other carrying a long gun. The hooves of their mounts drummed across the ground, the sound just reaching Lannigan.

'All of you listen!' Lannigan called. 'Slade's comin' in with twenty riders an' a wagon an' four. We'll let 'em come on, an' nobody shoots until I say so!'

He slid his Peacemaker from its holster, spinning the chamber to check again that it was fully loaded. Atop the bulk of timber before him were boxes of shells ready for a rapid reload. On his gunbelt were more shells for when he left the cover of the balcony and went down on Main Street.

By now Slade and his men could easily be seen with the naked eye, and Joe dropped to one knee behind the strengthened balcony. Two Winchester rifles, already loaded, were alongside him with boxes of shells on the floor of the balcony, and on his hip was a Colt.

'Sure hope I amount to somethin', Marshal,' Joe said softly, his head turned away from Lannigan in the direction of the approaching bunch of riders.

'It ain't gonna be a hoe-down, Joe,' Lannigan said. 'An' things'll maybe seem mighty slow to you when they're happenin'. But it's gonna be over and done with faster than you ever reckoned.'

Joe turned to raise his eyes to Lannigan. 'You ever been scared, Marshal?'

'Man who says he ain't ever been scared, Joe, is a damn liar, or a damn worse fool.'

Joe nodded, and reached down to

pick up one of the Winchesters, turning away from Lannigan to slide the barrel across the top of the balcony. He glanced briefly at Lannigan before turning away once more to sight along the barrel which he pointed steadily in the direction of Slade's oncoming men.

'July past I won a box of candy for shootin' this long gun,' he said, as if talking to himself. 'P'raps somebody should've told 'em.'

Lannigan, his eyes fixed on Slade and his riders, picked up the red cloth from where it was draped across the rail in front of him. He knew that if his plan was to work he had to get the timing of his signal just right. If he'd judged rightly he reckoned Slade and his men would start shooting as soon as they reached the edge of town, not caring what they hit, intent only on clearing a path down Main Street to the bank. Had Plainsville not been ready for them, Lannigan knew, Slade would have been through the doors of the bank while the townsfolk were still taking cover, and he and Charley Ford running along the boardwalk to find out what all the noise was about.

He could now hear the sound of the Bar-T driver shouting to the horses. Slade had been smart to use the wagon. Not only could it give protection if needed but Slade could also use it as a battering ram should anything get in his way. Sure, Slade had everything under tight control, but surprise was worth twenty guns, and it looked as if Slade's men were riding close enough for his own plan to work.

As the Bar-T riders broke from the rough ground of the trail to hit Main Street Lannigan held his hand high, clutching the red cloth. Fifty yards to run, he guessed. Shots rang out as Slade's men began to shoot ahead of them, the rapid firing of their long guns sounding briefly like the high-speed fire of a Gatling gun. Twenty-five yards. God help them all if his plan didn't work. Ten yards. He thumbed back the gunhammer of his Peacemaker, and filled his lungs with air. Then he brought down the red cloth, giving the signal to George and Sep Hardy to throw themselves against the rope rigged through Hardy's lifting blocks.

From the dusty soil ten yards ahead of the wagon the rope, tethered between buildings and lashed to the smithy's forge, sprung chest high to the horses. A wild shout of fear came from the wagon driver as he saw what was ahead. Throwing himself backwards against the seat he hauled on his reins, but he could do nothing to stop the headlong charge of the horses and they breasted the rope a few inches below their foaming mouths. For a terrible moment Lannigan thought that the momentum of their gallop and the weight of the wagon would send them bursting through. Then one of the leading horses stumbled.

In an instant the air was torn with the noise of wounded horses, as the leading pair went down, their tortured screams bouncing between the wooden buildings of the street. As Slade and the leading riders piled into the back of the wagon, it leapt forward in the air driving the two rear horses down to their knees. A human scream of terror rent the air as the driver was catapulted into the hurricane of flashing hooves and flying timber.

A wagon wheel hurtled across the street two feet above the ground and smashed on to the stout timbers at the edge of the boardwalk, rebounding to strike a wall, smashing the wood into splintered fragments. Behind the wagon, oaths and curses rang out as the two lines of riders telescoped, sending horses and men crashing down into the dirt of the street, already being stained with blood. Above the din of men and horses Lannigan's voice rang out across the street.

'Fire!'

For almost thirty seconds Lannigan, Kansas, and Joe sent bullets raining down on the street below them. Some of the riders at the rear of the Bar-T lines rolled from their mounts to run across the street only to be cut down by the deep throated blasts from the shotguns fired by Ford and Skinny.

Other Bar-T riders, shocked by the impact of their flesh on wood and metal, staggered around the street, attempting to reach shelter from the rapid fire which poured down upon them. Riderless horses ran around, eyes rolling in panic, terrified by the barrage of shooting.

Lannigan's eyes desperately searched for Slade among the few Bar-T riders, quicker in their reactions and perhaps with more courage than others, as they ran for cover, already twisting around to return fire from their rifles, sending splinters of wood flying around the balcony of the saloon. But the survivors of the onslaught were small in number and soon the street was littered with bodies. Lannigan saw that only a few men in the dirt of the street were still alive, their raised hands beating feebly at the air as if attempting to ward off the flying lead.

'Can you see Slade?' Lannigan shouted.

'He lost his horse! I reckon he made the alleyway by the store,' Joe shouted back, brass arcing through the air as he frantically levered his Winchester. Slugs hit the top of the wooden bulwarks sending splinters flying, and both Lannigan and Joe ducked down.

Joe's chest rose and fell. 'Maybe four of 'em in that alleyway,' he gasped. 'They've no way out.'

'Keep 'em pinned down, Joe! An' watch for my signal to stop firin'!'

Lannigan grabbed at another handful of shells, before covering the length of the balcony in a crouch, to run down the open stairway. As he reached the boardwalk he threw himself against the wall, taking cover from the slugs smacking into the wood around him. Then before his would-be killers could again take aim Lannigan hurtled off the boardwalk, and raced across the street. The wind of a slug brushed close to his face, the noise from a sidearm sounding close, and he flung himself behind a bulk of timber broken away from the wrecked wagon.

'Reckon there's three of 'em in that alleyway, Marshal!' Kansas shouted from above him.

Lannigan leaned back against the timber and spun the chamber of his Peacemaker. Joe had said four. How many were in the alleyway, four or three? He knew he'd never get back to the boardwalk alive if the men in the alleyway weren't stopped. And was Slade one of them? He knew he'd have to back Kansas. Two shots for each man against their three guns, and he'd be facing the alleyway blind. If the three were spread apart he'd maybe get two before the other had a chance to cut him down. He got to one knee and held up his left hand to shoulder level. He hoped to hell that Joe was still thinking right. If he missed his signal one of the slugs from Joe's Winchester would cut him down. Lannigan filled his lungs with air, thumbed back the gunhammer of his Peacemaker, and tensed his legs. Then he brought his hand down. At the same time he threw himself up and forward to land, legs braced, facing down the alley. His brain registered shadowy outlines, and his Peacemaker roared three times. He watched, as in a macabre dance of death the three men jerked back into the dirt of the alleyway, their hands clawing at the air, as each of their hearts exploded with a slug from Lannigan's six-gun.

'That's enough, Marshal! Fer crissakes that's enough!'

Lannigan whirled around, his Peacemaker at arm's length, swinging in a wide arc to cover the street. Where the hell was that voice coming from?

'It's OK, Marshal,' Ford shouted. 'Me and Skinny got 'em covered.'

As if to show Ford meant business there was the deep throated roar of one of the shotguns. Heavy shot rattled like stormrain against a building.

'I'm tellin' we're finished!' hollered

the voice. 'Don't shoot no more, we're comin' out.' There was a pause, and as Lannigan scanned the other side of the street, from around the side of a building over to his right, four men emerged, their hands high in the air.

'Middle of the street and down in the dirt,' shouted Lannigan, his Peacemaker held high, his arm extended in their direction. 'Don't anybody else show themselves!'

The men took hesitant steps away from the corner of the building, and Lannigan reloaded his Peacemaker by the fingertip feel of the slugs and his sidearm, not taking his eyes off the four men as they crossed to the middle of the street and dropped, cross-legged, to the dirt. Satisfied, he scanned the dozen or more bodies which lay on the ground among the wreckage of the wagon and the carcasses of the four horses. The three or four men who had been left alive now lay unmoving in the dirt. Nothing stirred in the street, and Lannigan felt his wire-taut muscles begin to relax. Then his whole body stiffened and he looked up to the saloon balcony from where a whoop of triumph had broken through the silence. Up on the front of the saloon, Joe stood outlined against the painted wood, his Winchester held high. Lannigan felt as if a giant hand had clutched at his gut. What the hell did the kid think he was doing?

Something moved suddenly to his left. He spun around, his Peacemaker roaring as he worked the trigger. But even as the sidearm bucked back against his hand he knew he was too late. The long gun in the hands of Slade's man cracked an instant before the two slugs from Lannigan blasted away the side of his head. Lannigan swung around to see Joe's rifle falling in a lazy curve to bounce from the saloon front into the street. Lannigan saw Joe clutching at his chest, blood spraying between his fingers. Then he slid down out of sight.

Behind Lannigan, feet sounded on

the boardwalk, and he spun around once more, dropping to one knee, his Peacemaker swinging through the air before him, his finger tightening on the trigger. Then he froze. Running towards him was Lucy Walker, the school marm, her hair wild, dirt marking her face, strangled sobs coming from her open mouth. Lannigan jumped to the boardwalk and caught her by the shoulders as she reached him.

'You goddamned little fool!' he bawled at her. 'You tryin' to get yourself killed?'

The girl was barely able to speak, tears were pouring down her cheeks. She babbled words which Lannigan failed to grasp, their meaning lost to him in a mental whirl of relief that he hadn't put a bullet through her. Then his relief was wiped out and a chill ran through him as he finally understood what she was trying to tell him.

'Where is she? Where's Slade taken Jane?' Lannigan shouted, his fingers digging into the girl's shoulders.

'The livery barn! He's trying to get a horse!'

'Here, Marshal!'

Lannigan looked around to see Skinny halfrunning across the street towards him, clutching the reins of a stray horse. Pushing the girl away from him, Lannigan jumped down from the boardwalk and threw himself into the saddle, snatching the reins from Skinny's hand.

'Charley! Take over here!' he shouted.

With a vicious tug he brought around the horse's head, and dug his spurs cruelly into the animal's flanks. All he could think of now was getting Jane away from Slade. And then he'd kill the sonovabitch.

14

As his horse reached the livery stable, Lannigan hauled on the reins, kicked his feet free of the stirrups, and rolled from the saddle. He slammed against the ground, rolling over and over in the dirt, feeling his Peacemaker bite into the flesh of his hip. His head scraped against a mound of grass, and his hat went skimming away. The force of his roll brought him to within a couple of yards of the stable wall, and he scrabbled forward on all fours, breathing heavily. Rising to one knee he placed his ear hard against the timber, straining to hear any noise within. From behind him the hooves of the horse he had ridden thudded away out of earshot, and shouts from the other end of town reached him faintly.

The shouts faded and he stiffened as above the rustle of straw kicked up by uneasy horses Lannigan heard a woman weeping and a rasping whisper. Jane and Slade were still in the barn! Rage ran through him burning his blood as if with a branding iron.

'Slade! You got the showdown you been lookin' for,' he shouted. 'We'll finish it out here!'

Immediately he rolled along the stable wall to duck behind a stout post. A heavy short gun roared inside the barn and a slug tore through the wood where a second before he'd been leaning. Chips of wood flew through the air, and dust flew up a few feet away from him as a slug smacked into the ground. A scream, high with fear, rang out, and was cut off by the sound of a vicious slap.

Lannigan filled his lungs, forcing himself to think clearly. Getting himself hogtied wasn't going to help Jane. Slade was gambling on her being his ticket to freedom. He'd drag her out of the barn and make a run for it. But a cat and mouse game across the plains wouldn't keep Jane alive. He knew that when Slade had no further use for Jane he'd kill her. Underneath the fancy suit and silk vest he was no different from the sidewinders he himself had been forced to kill with his bare hands down in Kansas. He had to stop Slade even if it cost him his own life. He had to think of some way of keeping Slade bottled up in the stable that would maybe give Jane a chance to get away.

From behind the wooden post, Lannigan looked up, turning over the odds in his mind. The sky sure looked blue to the north. But he didn't regret taking the chance to settle his debts with Henry. His life since the War Between the States had been a good one, save for the trouble he'd had in Dodge. A damned shame he hadn't met Jane Hermann before, though. A woman like her got a man to thinking of settling down. He moved to rest on one knee, laid his Peacemaker on the ground, and unbuckled his gunbelt, letting it fall to the ground alongside his sidearm.

'Slade! I'm comin' in unarmed!' he shouted. 'No tricks, you have my word!'

'No, Studs!' Jane Hermann screamed. 'He'll kill you!'

Her voice was cut off by another vicious slap as Lannigan edged along the wall and pushed open the door. He moved quickly away from the light which he knew must have outlined him in the doorway.

On the floor near to him lay the unconscious figure of Jackson, blood pouring from a head wound. Ten yards beyond, beside a horse loosely tethered to the bar across an empty stall, stood Slade and Jane. The cotton fabric of her dress was torn at the shoulder revealing white skin marked with bruises, and across the side of her face, through streaks of dirt, angry marks showed where Slade had slapped her. Blood trickled from a cut on her lip, tracing a thin line down her chin. Slade held her hard against his body, his arm around her neck. In his other hand was his Peacemaker, the barrel aiming directly at Lannigan's heart.

'Get over here, Lannigan,' Slade rasped.

'Let the girl go first.'

'Do as you're goddamned told! Or I'll show you what I'm gonna do to this crazy bitch!'

With a slow tread, Lannigan passed down the line of horses towards Slade. When he was closer he could see Jane's eyes more clearly. They were wide with fear but maybe they still carried a gleam of defiance. He looked back to Slade and he could now see blood oozing down his left cheek from four deep scratches.

'Seems the lady's been doin' stuff to you, Slade.'

'Shut your goddamned mouth! You've been talkin' too much ever since you came to Plainsville,' Slade rasped. 'You're gonna lose this one, Lannigan. Two goddamned years I've worked this

240

country and I ain't leavin' empty-handed. You understan' me, you Yankee bastard?'

Almost as if they were alone together in the barn the two men stared fixedly at each other, and Lannigan saw the gleam of triumph in Slade's eyes, and tasted in his mouth the bitter bile of failure. In the past he'd played low cards and still walked away with the pot, but this time it looked as if he'd lost the game. But he hadn't thrown in his hand. For how much time Jane had, she'd know that. Once he'd enjoyed his triumph to the full Slade intended to kill him and there was nothing he could do about it. Deliberately, he turned his gaze away from Slade to look once more into Jane's green eyes.

'Yeah, look at her, you damn Yankee!' Slade rasped. 'But I'm gonna take her!'

Jane dropped her head and sank her teeth into the soft flesh of Slade's wrist and at the same time threw her legs forward, pulling Slade off balance. Lannigan snatched at the short-handled whip clipped to the side of the nearest stall, and lashed down at Slade's wrist, sending the Peacemaker spinning into the shadows. Cursing, Slade threw Jane away from him, sending her sprawling across the barn among horses which whinnied and stamped. Then he and Lannigan closed on each other, kicking and gouging, their hands curved into claws as they fought to gain a hold on the other's throat.

Slade stumbled in the thick straw, and Lannigan grasped his chance. With both hands clenched together, he swung his fists in a wide arc, and hammered at the side of Slade's neck. But even as his fists connected he felt Slade roll away from the blow, saw him drop for an instant to one knee, before springing up to sink a fist into Lannigan's kidneys as he, too, stumbled in the straw. Pain tore through Lannigan's body and he swallowed rapidly as vomit flooded the base of his throat. He saw Slade's clawed hands reaching for his throat and he spun sideways and lashed out at his knee. The leather of his heeled boot slammed against bone, and Slade's face turned ashen as he went staggering back several yards against the wall of the stable.

Lannigan leapt forward, his bunched fist held high, but saw he'd driven Slade back against the wall only to provide him with a new weapon. Through the sweat pouring down over his eyes he saw Slade snatch up a hayfork from against the stable wall. Backing away, Lannigan desperately looked around for a weapon of his own. He jumped aside in an attempt to snatch at the wooden bar across a stall but was cut off as the prongs of the hayfork flashed towards him. Lips pulled back from his teeth, Slade pushed himself off against the wall and moved forwards, dragging his damaged leg, the pole of the hayfork thrust forward, the sharpened prongs moving in a slow arc in front of Lannigan's body.

Lannigan started to retreat, slowly at first, then trying to move faster across the uneven ground as Slade began to trust his damaged leg and quicken his advance. Lannigan took another pace backwards and, too late, felt his boot slide on something loose below the straw. For an instant his arms flailed the air, as he fought to keep his balance while the hayfork prongs danced before him. His right heel gave way beneath him and he crashed to the straw-covered floor on his back, as Slade, a wolf-like gleam in his eyes, leapt forward to stab downwards at his chest.

Lannigan writhed across the ground, the prongs burying themselves into the straw only inches from his body, and he scrabbled for purchase on the ground with his knees and hands. His fingers closed around something hard and loose below the straw. Above him, scenting victory, Slade held the hayfork high again, steadying himself to plunge the prongs downwards into Lannigan.

Again, Lannigan rolled away, tensed his shoulder, and with the loose length of chain which had brought him down clenched within his fist, he lashed up at Slade's face. The heavy iron links whipped past the hayfork pole and smashed into the side of Slade's head, tearing the flesh. Blood spurted through the air, and with a strangled cry, Slade dropped the hayfork and staggered backwards, clutching at his eye.

Scrambling to his feet Lannigan saw Slade fall to the straw, pulling up his knees in an animal-like effort to ease his agony. As Slade slumped against the side of a stall Lannigan snatched up the hayfork, and with the back of a sweat-soaked hand, brushed away the blood which threatened to blind him. From beneath Slade's bowed head there came a torrent of muffled curses as the blood poured down through his fingers to blacken the material of his breeches.

If Slade knew Lannigan was standing before him he made no move to lift his head. He was like a beaten coyote, waiting for a stronger animal to deliver the fatal thrust, one of his hands clamped against his head, the other fluttering uselessly around the top of his boot. Lannigan raised the hayfork. Shooting was too good for this animal who had threatened to kill Jane. He spat blood at the bowed head to clear his mouth, steadied his feet and raised the hayfork higher, the pole held in his clenched fists above his head.

He stood poised, his chest heaving, battered and bloody in victory over a man who had destroyed the lives of good people, and who had driven Henry Hudson to his grave. And Lannigan knew then that if he brought the hayfork down he'd be no better than Slade. Deliberately, he lowered the hayfork and threw it aside into a pile of straw.

He spat the words at the bloodied head. 'You're gonna face a judge, Slade, an' I'll be around to see you hang.'

He turned away. Where was Jane? All he wanted now was to make sure she was safe. His eyes searched the shadows, the sweat and blood around his eyes hindering his efforts to focus on the length of the stable.

'No!' Jane's scream rang out, and Lannigan spun around to look back at Slade.

What he saw froze him to the ground. Slade had raised his head, his face a double-sided gory mask. From one side blood poured from his torn eye and the shredded flesh of his cheek. From the other, a yellow eye gleamed with triumph between narrowed lids. In his hand Slade held a Derringer which he must have pulled, Lannigan realized, from the top of his boot. The small black hole at the end of the pistol's barrel seemed to swamp Lannigan's vision. At this range, Slade couldn't miss.

Slade brought the pistol to aim at Lannigan's heart. Below the yellow eye, the corner of his mouth pulled up in a snarl.

'See you in hell, Lannigan,' he said, and pulled the trigger.

As the pistol barked there came from

behind Lannigan the loud report of a heavy short gun. Lannigan saw Slade's yellow eye explode in a star of blood and his head smash back against the wall. His body toppled over into the straw, quivered for a moment, and then lay still.

Lannigan swung around. A few feet away in the centre of the stable stood Jane, Slade's Peacemaker dangling from her fingers down beside the skirt of her torn dress. Her head was thrown back, her mouth wide open, and, as Lannigan watched, her eyes rolled back in her head, and she folded noiselessly to the ground.

15

Lannigan, with a touch on Dollar's reins, brought the buggy around to the track leading to the two-storeyed building which stood alone two miles out of town. Above his new black boots he wore a grey broadcloth suit, his badge showing on the creamcoloured shirt beneath his jacket. Between his feet on the floor of the buggy lay his gunbelt. Alongside him sat Jane in a blue silk dress, a band of black crêpe an inch or so above her left elbow.

'I'm sure glad you made this trip with me, Jane,' Lannigan said. 'I ain't sure how Jed Martin's gonna receive me.'

Jane placed her hand on Lannigan's arm, as he brought Dollar to a halt close to the high wooden steps below the main door of Jed Martin's fine house. Lannigan jumped out, hitched Dollar to the rail, and then moved back to hand down Jane from the buggy. As he did so Jed Martin appeared at the open door beyond the top of the steps. A stiff collar held his chin firm above his stringy neck and his watery blue eyes peered short-sightedly at them as they went up the steps.

'Miss Hermann,' he said bending forward to Jane in an old-fashioned bow. 'Marshal. Good of you both to come.'

The elderly man moved aside to allow them to enter the silent house, and Lannigan took off his pearl-grey Stetson.

'Would you care to see him?' asked Martin in a voice which trembled slightly.

Lannigan nodded, feeling Jane grasp at the cuff of his jacket. Together, they followed Jed Martin along a corridor bordered by white stone walls on which hung three old paintings from a distant country. Jed Martin led them along polished floorboards until he reached a closed door, where he looked back as if making sure they had followed him. He slowly pushed open the door, and again stood back to allow them to enter. In the centre of the room Lannigan saw the afternoon sun streaming through the window on to the alabaster-white face of Joe Martin.

Slowly, Lannigan and Jane moved to stand alongside the bed and look down at Joe's face. His eyes opened slowly.

'Marshal? Is that you?'

Lannigan could barely hear him. He bent forward, aware that Jane was still gripping his sleeve. 'Sure is, trooper. And Miss Jane's with me.'

Lannigan waited while Joe struggled to speak. 'Doc Evans says I'm gonna make it,' he managed to whisper.

'Sure you are, Joe,' Lannigan said. 'Your gran'pa needs you, an' so does Plainsville. A year or two you're gonna be a big man around these parts.'

Joe's lips moved fractionally upwards. 'Guess I'll learn to obey orders first.'

Jed Martin looked down at his grandson. 'Doc Evans says Joe's gonna be fine, though he'll ache mighty bad for a couple winters.' A smile appeared on his lined face. 'I'm mighty proud of him.'

'We'll be back again soon, Joe,' Jane said.

Lannigan stood gazing down at the young man whose eyes had closed again. 'Me and Henry sure could have done with you at Wilderness,' he said. But he saw Joe hadn't heard him, the young man's chest rising and falling steadily in sleep.

'I'd like to offer you coffee,' Jed Martin said, as they returned along the white-walled corridor.

'Thanks Mr Martin, but I must meet the stage. There's feller comin' into town who's gonna clear up a mystery for me,' Lannigan said.

Outside the house, at the top of the steps, he shook hands with Jed Martin who again bowed to Jane. A minute or two later the buggy drew away from the house and Lannigan and Jane both turned and waved to the elderly man who stood watching their departure.

As the buggy rattled along the short track leading from the house and Lannigan buckled on his gunbelt, he and Jane were silent with their thoughts. Dollar, trotting steadily, hauled the buggy through the wide gateposts, and on to the path leading back to town. They were fifty yards off the Martin property when Lannigan broke the silence.

'I still feel bad about that kid.'

Jane tossed her head, her red hair moving off the nape of her neck in a gesture of impatience. 'Honestly! Joe's alive because Doc Evans got to him quickly and that was your doing. Charley Ford's walking tall again. Skinny and the rest are being treated as heroes, and the town's stronger for having survived.'

'What'll happen out at the ranch?' Lannigan asked. 'Now that your brother's gone.'

Jane fell silent, glancing down at the crêpe on her arm. 'I'll always have

253

happy memories of Jimmy,' she said finally. 'He was hotheaded, and sometimes he acted foolishly but when those rotten gunslingers threatened our Mexican girls Jimmy stood up and fought like a real man.'

Lannigan flicked the whip over Dollar's head to turn him from the track, and Jane put a hand on his arm again to steady herself as the buggy gained the hard ground of the trail into town.

'How's your pa taking it?' Lannigan asked when the buggy had settled again.

'He's grieving, of course, but he's recovering from his wounds, thank God.' Jane's sombre expression was replaced by a smile. 'He's enjoying having Amy Powell fuss about him.'

Lannigan grinned. 'An' I hear that she ain't exactly uncomfortable fussin' him. I reckon they'll not be arguin' over Lisher's four years in the Cavalry and Beaver Creek, no matter what your pa's lawyer says.'

Jane's eyes shone. 'That old villain's far too occupied to worry about a homestead! Father has him busy making matters right with the towns-people.' Her expression changed and she bit her lip. 'Slade did some terrible things in my father's name.'

Lannigan reached out and squeezed her hand. 'Decent folks ain't slow to forgive. Your pa'll soon be a welcome face in Plainsville again.'

'I hope so.' She looked away down Main Street suddenly, as the buggy left the trail. 'The stage is already in town! Aren't you expecting someone?'

'Sure am.' Lannigan flicked the whip above Dollar who increased his pace to haul the buggy towards the stage office, where the stage stood being unloaded. Several people called out their greetings from the boardwalks. A cluster of rangemen around the smithy shouted their good wishes. Jane gave them a happy smile, and there was a burst of cheering from the men.

'Cowboys always did admire a pretty

girl,' said Lannigan with a grin. He pointed with his whip at a tall man standing alongside the coach watching his bags being unloaded by a couple of youngsters. Lannigan halted Dollar as Skinny crossed the street towards them.

'Take care of the buggy for me. I need a word with Mr McParlen.'

'Sure thing, Marshal. Charley's about the town.'

Skinny held Dollar's head while Jane took Lannigan's hand to step down from the buggy, her free hand lifting her skirts clear of the street. Lannigan heard the Irishman giving orders for his luggage to be taken to the hotel, and saw him throw coins to the youngsters. From their shouts Lannigan guessed McParlen had been generous. As Skinny led away the buggy, McParlen turned and walked towards them, his hand lifted to raise his hat in the direction of Jane.

'Good to see you, Miss Hermann.' McParlen replaced his hat, and warmly shook Lannigan's hand. 'How are you,

Marshal? Better than the last time I saw you, I'm bound to say!'

Lannigan studied McParlen's face. Beneath that Irish smile he knew there was a sharp brain at work.

'We need to talk, Mr McParlen,' he said.

'I expected to, Marshal. Perhaps you'll join me at the hotel later?'

'There's no time like now,' Lannigan said. 'An' we can talk in my office.'

McParlen nodded his head in agreement. 'And Miss Hermann . . . ?' he queried.

'I guess she's as much right as anyone to know what's been going on,' Lannigan said.

'Then I'll be pleased to accompany you both,' McParlen said.

A few minutes later the three of them were seated around Lannigan's desk. A boy had brought them coffee from the hotel in blue china cups stamped with the hotel's name. The Irishman lowered his cup to the saucer standing at the edge of Lannigan's desk.

'How far did you get with the shooting of Monroe?' McParlen asked.

'Hold on there, Mr McParlen,' Lannigan said, his grin taking the sting out of the words. 'You mind tellin' me right off just what your business is with folks 'round here?'

McParlen shrugged. 'No harm in telling now, Marshal. I'm a Pinkerton detective, hired by Union Pacific.'

He reached into a deep pocket in his jacket, and laid identification papers on the desk. 'UP likes to make sure about a town before it brings in the railroad. Folks back East with the money were becomin' fidgety. Plainsville was getting known for the wrong sort of reasons, and they wanted to know what was goin' on.'

He looked away towards Jane, who gazed back at him, showing no emotion, before turning back towards Lannigan. 'Guess I can now tell UP that Plainsville's been tamed, and they can bring in the branch line without worryin'.'

Lannigan picked up the papers from the desk and read them quickly. Satisfied, he passed them back to McParlen, and paused for a while, getting his own thoughts in order.

'OK, now I'll answer your question. I reckon Monroe was plannin' some sort of deal with Bart Hermann over the land around Beaver Creek. He must have got hold of the Homesteader's Certificate when Lisher died.'

Lannigan glanced briefly at Jane before continuing. 'I reckon Slade saw Monroe as a threat an' decided to have him killed. I'm guessin' now, but I reckon Monroe was shot the mornin' of the day he meant to meet with Bart Hermann, an' Slade's men left him for dead when they couldn't find the papers hidden in his boot.'

He paused again, his thoughts going back to that first day by Beaver Creek, getting the scene back into his mind. 'First time I saw Monroe's horse it was lathered with sweat, an' I reckon Monroe must have been makin' for town when he ran out of time.'

'So was he shot out at the Bar-T?' McParlen asked.

Lannigan shook his head. 'I don't reckon so. My guess is Slade's men caught him at dawn up in the high meadows to the south-west. While I was out ridin' I found a campfire that wasn't all that old.'

'And you reckon it was Monroe's camp?'

Lannigan shrugged. 'I'll never be sure, but there were bloodstains on the grass up there.' He smiled wryly at McParlen. 'Anyways, the camp was in a meadow full of wild daisies.'

A beaming smile spread across McParlen's face. 'Excellent, Mr Lannigan, excellent.' He picked up his papers from the desk, pushed them into a pocket, and then from another pocket took a single sheet of paper. He read it quickly, apparently checking its contents, then turned it around, and placed it on the desk in front of Lannigan.

Lannigan frowned. 'What's all this about?'

'I guess it's about more money than you've ever earned in your life, Marshal. Sign that paper, and you're a Pinkerton agent.'

For several seconds Lannigan looked down at the single sheet of paper. Some mighty strange happenings had come his way lately. And some of them he could have done without, that was for sure. But this wasn't one of them. He read the wording of the Pinkerton offer again. Working for the outfit started by Alan Pinkerton sure did things for a man's standing, as good almost as working for the Government people back East. Down in Texas when he wore a sheriff's badge he'd come across Pinkerton agents. They lived in fine hotels, wore fancy clothes, had plenty of money for guns and ammunition. They drank decent whiskey and ate good grub. And they didn't spend their time throwing drunken cowboys out of saloons. A man might be thought foolish to turn down a chance like this. He picked up the paper, and handed it back to McParlen.

'I'm mighty grateful, Mr McParlen, but I'll have to pass on this.'

The Irishman took the paper. 'I had to try, Marshal. I guess Plainsville'll not be looking too far when the judge in Cheyenne appoints a sheriff.'

Lannigan shook his head. 'Plainsville's gonna need a new man. Somebody who'll collect taxes, an' make sure the youngsters get to school. That ain't for me. Time somebody else wore this badge. Anyways, I got these kinfolk . . . '

Jane interrupted, speaking for the first time since the two men had begun to discuss the previous days. 'Mr Lannigan will be too busy running the Bar-T to wear a badge any more,' she said.

Lannigan turned towards her, aware that he was staring at Jane as if seeing her for the first time. Hadn't he already told Bart Hermann a couple of times that punching cattle wasn't for him? Then he caught McParlen's knowing glance, and his amused smile. How did the Pinkerton man know more about this than he did, or was McParlen just faster at working things out?

'If the marshal'll not work for the Pinkerton Agency Miss Hermann, how d'you reckon he'll work for you?' McParlen said, his smile growing broader.

'He'll not be working for anyone, Mr McParlen,' Jane said, her green eyes shining. She stood up from her chair and moved around to stand beside Lannigan whose expression was that of a man not quite sure what was happening to him.

'Mr Lannigan and I are to be married shortly,' she said, placing her hand on his shoulder. 'Apart from my father and Amy Powell you're the first to be told.'

There was a moment of total silence while Lannigan looked straight across the desk at McParlen as if he wasn't sure of his next words.

'An' that's a darn sight truer than you'll ever reckon, Mr McParlen,' he said finally. A broad grin lit up his weatherbeaten face, and he reached up to cover Jane's hand with his own. 'Sure is a surprisin' town around here, ain't it?'

THE END

95742

THE CHISELLER

Tex Larrigan

Soon the paddle-steamer would be on its long journey down the Missouri River to St Louis. Now, all Saul Rhymer had to do was to play the last master-stroke of the evening. He looked at the mounting pile of gold and dollar bills and again at the cards in his hand. Then, looking around the table, he produced the deed to the goldmine in Montana. 'Let's play poker!' But little did he know how that journey back to St Louis would change his life so drastically.